OK
BEST

OK BEST

A Collection of Short Stories

**A Project of Full Circle Bookstore
and Individual Artists of Oklahoma**

A Project of Full Circle Bookstore and Individual Artists of Oklahoma

To maintain the authentic style of each writer included in *OK Best: A Collection of Short Stories*, certain quirks of spelling and grammar remain unchanged from their original state.

Project Coordinators: Kelly Ross Jump
                    Angela S. Smith
                    Shauna Lawyer Struby

Edited by Kelly Ross Jump and Libby Price
Book design by Carl Brune
Cover photograph by Tom Lee

Printed and bound in the United States of America.

Published by
Full Circle Bookstore
50 Penn Place
Oklahoma City, Oklahoma.

ISBN: 0-9661460-0-x

Special Thanks

A project of this magnitude could not possibly happen without the assistance of many. Special thanks to those mentioned below who so graciously and generously gave of their time.

Readers

These ten brave souls spent countless hours reading and scoring the 256 entries, all without compensation.

Paul Bailey

David Clark

Mike Easterling

Marsha Lowry

Gaylene Murphy

Jason Nelson

Valerie Saad

Sandra Soli

Nancy Struby

Ginnie Tack

The Board of Directors, IAO Performance Committee and staff of IAO for assistance, support and encouragement.

Tom Lee, for generously donating his photograph for the cover of *OK Best*.

Our juror, Stewart O'Nan, for advice, help and encouragement above and beyond the call of duty.

Robyn Arn and Rurie Miller for assistance in planning and executing.

Spontaneous Bob for assistance with publicity.

Contents

Preface

There are two kinds of dreams, the waking and the sleeping. Sometimes the two are the same. Almost two years ago I stood in the crowded museum store at the Dallas Museum of Art and thumbed through a collection of short stories by Texas writers.

I remember then wishing somebody would produce such a collection for the talented writers of Oklahoma. It was a waking dream that invaded my sleep—a wistful thought that refused to be forgotten. The challenge of the dream—find an avenue for Oklahoma voices.

A few months later the way became clear when a casual remark I made over a spicy Thai lunch produced the partnership that lead to this collection. The synchronicity of that moment still amazes me.

I couldn't have asked for a better partner than Full Circle Bookstore. Their commitment and genuine love of literature has made this an enjoyable adventure. Special thanks to all those who have made *OK Best* a reality: the volunteer readers, the staff at IAO, Angela Smith of IAO's Performance Committee, our illustrious juror, Stewart O'Nan, all the writers who submitted work, and a very special thank you to Kelly Ross Jump of Full Circle Bookstore, whose unending patience truly astounds me.

Dreams do really come true. For Oklahoma writers—this book proves it.

Shauna Lawyer Struby
Individual Artists of Oklahoma

What started as a conversation over lunch has culminated in this inaugural collection of stories. Along the way we have learned many lessons and hopefully found the courage for improvement. I hope you will find this labor of love a testament to the talent of writers living in Oklahoma.

My thanks to the over 150 writers who submitted, and my congratulations to the 12 who were chosen. I would also like to thank the ten devoted readers who volunteered for the thankless job of culling out the submissions. Finally, I would like to give a very special thanks to Stewart O'Nan for graciously serving as our final judge. Together you have left us an intriguing choir of Oklahoma voices.

Angela S. Smith
Individual Artists of Oklahoma

Full Circle has consistently focused our promotional activities and in-store events on Oklahoma authors. In the course of developing our 1996 event plan, Kelly Jump (Full Circle's newsletter editor, special events coordinator and primary marketing person) and I talked longingly about the feasibility of Full Circle publishing a book of short stories, written by our talented customers and friends, but we had felt our resources would be challenged by the logistics.

Then the Bookstore God smiled, and Kelly discovered that Shauna and the IAO shared our dream, and the publication of *OK Best* was assured. It just was a matter of time, enormous effort by the IAO volunteers, Stewart O'Nan's perceptive (and fearless) selection of the thirteen best stories, the application of book designer Carl Brune's remarkable talent, and great commitment by Kelly and Libby Price (Full Circle's resident critic). My role was to say yes, make a small investment, and forever call myself a publisher.

We of course want to sell many copies of *OK Best*, but our real pleasure is bringing these twelve talented authors to your attention . . . You can read a lot into the title *OK Best*.

James R. Tolbert III
Full Circle Bookstore

These Thirteen

In choosing these thirteen stories for *OK Best*, I had one standard, the one most readers subscribe to: interest. If the story was interesting, I took it. I wasn't looking for stories to fulfill themes, promote local color or champion a certain mode of writing I feel is healthiest for American (or any) fiction. And that may explain why this collection goes all over the place in tone, style and subject matter.

Look at Paul Burke's "Sunday Morning." While it seems to mimic the clipped, domestic fiction so many critics labeled minimalism, as the story progresses it ventures into a surreal realm readers of Julio Cortazar's "House Taken Over" will recognize and delight in. It's at once understated and in-your-face, relying on a kind of deadpan terror.

I've put Robert Hibbard's "Bottles" right on the heels of "Sunday Morning" to emphasize the weirdness of his hero Parsons's daily existence. While this might easily be mistaken for '80s trailer park fiction—the extreme close-up on the mundane—Hibbard's attention to language makes Parsons's world spark and crackle, gives a story readers may think they're familiar with an unexpected bite.

And then Christopher Forrest Givan's "Hamlet in Texas" stretches out and gives us a partially self-conscious, possibly even mad narrator who sees invisible and inane connections between everything and delivers drop-dead summaries of his life so far. The irony, which could overwhelm the piece, turn too cute, is leavened by our speaker being unaware of his strange take on things.

Jim Drummond's "Archangelsk" also opens with a literary (and pop) reference, then moves immediately into a daring and completely winning metaphor worthy of Nabokov, and just barrels on from there, sucking in puns, absurdly named characters and the detritus of the last hundred years of high and low culture. And then when we're exhausted keeping up with it all, wondering what this sprawl means, Drummond stops short, turns and throws down a mini-SAT like Trey Ellis in *Platitudes* and finds a satisfying ending. This is metafiction at its best: wild, thought-provoking and fun—a real carnival ride.

"Honorable Discharge," also by Jim Drummond, takes us further into the bizarre, compressing language and image to create jarring, poetic effects. At times it's clear and simple, its repetition comforting as old Hemingway; at others it's totally elusive, so opaque it's almost closed off. And what to make of the collision of the Emperor Jones and Tina Turner near the end? The Alabama National Guard? I'm not sure myself, but I like what it does to me. Sometimes you've just got to roll with it.

If "Honorable Discharge" takes us way out there, Laura Holcomb McNatt's "The Trip" brings us back. Here are the eternal verities, the certainties of character and action clearly drawn and leisurely paced as the lives of these two older women. This is the standard psychological realism we call mainstream, the tone reminiscent of Eudora Welty's "A Worn Path," a civility and humor harkening back to the stories of the great Peter Taylor.

And right behind it waits Joan K. Moore's "The Marriage Question," which flies by, daring you to catch up. Again, there's compression, elision, lightning-quick metaphor. The reader is asked to make connections, to follow the narrative as it hurtles through a maze of reversals as the speaker's tangle of lies and envy falls apart. It's fast, sure work and never lets you get comfortable.

"Life, Love, Marriage, Dental Molds" by Steffie Corcoran is its opposite: deliberately paced, heavy on set piece exposition, and purely chronological, its scenes laid out plainly. It's playful and sad and funny, a soft spoof of middle-aged love that might come from Jill McCorkle or Lawrence Naumoff.

Set against such a conventionally rendered story, the abrupt time shifts and sudden striking imagery of Linda Marshall Sigle's "Violin Music in the Night" seems even more powerful. The narrator recounts her disturbing past with a poet's eye and ear and leaves us wondering about her unsteady present. Examine how deftly the author takes us through the years, places us vividly in the different settings—yet there are almost no fully rendered scenes.

Benjamin Bates's "Produce" juxtaposes the narrator's wild dreams against his mundane, oddly comic life. In a brilliant, versatile performance, Bates conjures both palpable dream images (very difficult) and believable sustained dialogues (even tougher). Our narrator is a complex presence; we can feel his not-so-pure desires. And which is more absurd, his guest shot on Oprah or his dream of her?

In "Musubi," Amanda Price pushes language hard in the beginning, giving us the wonderful trilogy of "birthing, pork chops, and Bible study" as if these things naturally fit with each other. There is only one full scene here, but the principals are given the room and the ability to make their larger relationships clear to the reader, and their views of the world are sharp, even cutting.

At first Paul Bowers's "Taking Certain Measures" could also be mistaken for trailer park or minimalist fiction—in its focus on yardwork, domestic and neighborly relations— but early into the second page the reader understands that our narrator is a bit too gifted verbally and maybe a little too excited (interested, yes, very) about everything around him. By page five, he's knocking out heavy-duty sentences like, "The water rose in high silver arches before shattering into wet confetti." The story gets both more plain and stranger the deeper you get into it.

And finally, Brooks Tower's "Song of So" takes the actual construction of itself as its titular subject. It's a true virtuoso performance, utterly baroque, always threatening to collapse under the weight of its rather heavy conceits and showy language yet always finding a way to astonish us again, take sudden flight. Like "Archangelsk," it's in-your-face, brazen in demanding your complicity and, in the end, thoroughly winning.

If forced to, I could probably pair a few of these thirteen stories up, maybe put one group of three together that have superficial similarities. It's a real shotgun collection, which is good, I think. What I've liked most about working with and reading emerging writers is the variety of experience and expression they possess. I noticed this at the University of Central Oklahoma, and I noticed it in the selections I read for this anthology.

And it's not just Oklahoma; this explosion of form and style is happening everywhere, and at every level. I'm not sure what's behind it, other than the natural adventurousness and daring of writers, both those writing now and those who've left us such a wild and powerful legacy, but I'm glad to be around to read such interesting work. I hope you find these stories as challenging and satisfying, as strange and familiar as I do. I think they speak well of the state of the art in Oklahoma and the state of the art across the nation.

Stewart O'Nan

Sunday Morning

Paul Burke

"Who are they?" Roger asked. He stood in the kitchen, empty coffee cup in hand. His bathrobe was rumpled, his shock of hair uncombed. Tamera, his wife, sat at the kitchen table reading the newspaper. She did not look up.

"Who are who?" she asked, flipping one page then another.

"Who are those children playing in the den?"

"I don't know," she said. "I thought you knew them."

"I don't know them. You're not baby-sitting or something?"

"God, no."

"Then how did they get in here?"

"They rang the doorbell," she said. "I let them in. I thought you knew them."

"I don't know them."

"I know that now." Tamera tapped a finger on her horoscope and sighed.

Roger scowled into his coffee cup. Stepping past his wife, he filled his coffee, filled hers while he was at it, then sat down at the kitchen table.

"This is strange," he said.

"Strange," Tamera said.

"We need to find out who they are," he said.

"I guess so," Tamera said.

Roger tested the coffee to his lips. Too hot. He stirred in some more sugar. "How many are there? Children, that is."

"Thirty-seven."

"That's an awful lot of children."

"Yes," she said. "You want part of the paper?"

"No. You finish it." Roger never liked getting just part of the paper. He wanted the entire paper all at once, then he would order it to his choosing, read everything, and never touch the paper again. Tamera knew this. He thought she might be taunting him.

"I'm done with it, really," she said. She pushed a mass of newspaper towards him. "I'm going to get a book out of the den."

Tamera left the table, and Roger began to restack the paper. He hated Sundays. They had a nasty, confusing feel about them, one that he couldn't quite put his finger on. He assumed it was because he and Tamera didn't wake up together. Every other day, even Saturdays, they woke up together. They had been doing so for ten years and had become pretty good at it. On Sundays, though, left to each's own pace, Tamera was always up before Roger. She would read the paper first, drink the coffee first, and, almost always, do something entirely inappropriate. Last Sunday, she installed blue vinyl siding on their neo-Victorian home. Another time, she built a crucifix out of chicken wire and roses and insisted on entering it into a parade. Although allowing thirty-seven strange children to rifle through Roger's den was comparatively mild and required no tools, Tamera knew that he preferred to read the paper in the den. Besides, those kids could want a snack at anytime, and all that was in the refrigerator were four cans of herring that Roger was saving for lunch.

Tamera returned from the den carrying an armload of thick books. "Art books," she announced. "Brueghel, Van Gogh, Monet—all the biggies." They made a dull thud when she dropped them to the table. Coffee sloshed over the rim of Roger's cup onto his freshly ordered paper— real estate on top, comics on bottom, other sections arranged in varying degrees of momentary interest.

"What the hell are those for?" he asked, trying not to sound snide while he dribbled coffee from his paper back into its cup.

"I'm going to write my memoirs," she said. She took her seat and plucked the Brueghel book from the stack.

"Did you find out who those children are?"

"Was I supposed to do that?"

"Never mind," Roger said, and he turned his attention to his paper. The "Dream Home of The Week" had a wet brown splotch across its stucco exterior. The text was beginning to run. He tried to read around the spill until it occurred to him that thirty-seven children should have been making a lot more noise than was being made.

"They sure are quiet," he said. "The children, that is."

"Yes. Quiet."

"What are they doing?"

"Building a fort on top of the piano. Well, some of them are building a fort. The rest are digging a bunker near the fireplace. They're going to play war."

"Can't they do that outside?"

"It's too nice outside. War is dark and ugly. I drew the curtains for them and put red hankies over the lamps. Oh, look at this." Tamera pushed the book across the table and turned it so Roger could see. He looked down onto a very colorful plate full of demonic creatures and screaming women.

"Nice," he said. When he picked up his coffee, he purposely caused some to spill onto the page. "Sorry."

Tamera's face turned as quiet and dull as if she had just woken up on a Tuesday morning. Pulling the book back to her, she began to dab at the spill with a cascade of hair off her shoulder. Her hair was thick and dark, twisting wildly from her head to somewhere near her waist. Years ago, Roger had dreamed he had climbed her hair (he was very small in the dream) and had discovered near her left ear a tiny village, a replica of his own town, really, with a tiny movie theater and a tiny Wal-Mart and a tiny neo-Victorian house just like his. Theirs. And Tamera was there too, in the same scale miniature as he, but he was climbing her hair, so he was suddenly smaller, climbing the hair of the smaller Tamera, and near her left ear was a tiny village, and she was there, too, but he was climbing her hair, etc. He kept climbing smaller and smaller versions of Tamera's hair up to smaller and smaller versions of Tamera's ear until the original Tamera cast a gigantic shadow, and he woke up. Suddenly. He woke up and turned to his wife to make sure she was her normal size, but she was not in bed.

That was on a Sunday, too. He had searched for her that morning, wandering naked through their neo-Victorian home and eventually found her in the backyard, also naked, planting a garden of eggplant and cabbage. "But I don't like eggplant," he told her.

"Who does?" she had said, and she ran a muddy hand through her mass of hair. When she did, Roger, not completely awake, flinched, imagining the entire village with him and even Tamera being swiped from her ear and crashing to the ground.

That was rather how he felt now. That was how Sundays felt, like he was falling, always falling. How did he, they, even make it through a week? Watching her twirl a coffee soaked strand of hair between her fingers, Roger thought, "I can't face another Sunday. Not like this. Not with you."

He was about to tell his wife the same thing when a chorus of trumpets sounded from the den. A plume of smoke filled the hallway. There was a small explosion, then a bigger explosion, and Tamera sprang from her chair. Roger stood, too, mimicking his wife, but before he could adjust his robe, an army of sandy-headed, orange-clad children burst into the kitchen wielding foam rubber bats, plastic spears, and small, automatic pistols. Their screeches were deafening:

"We're hungry!"

"Where's the bathroom?"

"He pushed me!"

"We're hungry!"

There might have been thirty-seven. Roger didn't get a chance to count. A series of body blocks soon sent him to his knees where he was forced to grasp the back of his chair to keep from falling over completely. Some of the children began to Indian wrestle on the table, scattering books and newspaper, or they pulled metal things out of the lower cabinets. Others ignited small fires on the stove and counter tops with disposable lighters. Roger scanned the fray for Tamera, but she appeared to be missing.

He pulled himself up and called for Tamera, but no answer came back. She had either escaped or was being pummeled under that group of kids gathered near the espresso machine. He could at least save the herring, he thought, but when he made a move towards the refrigerator, he was felled by a head butt to the kidneys. Once down, several sticky hands began pulling at his face and hair. A chant went up: "Roger is a Frogger! Roger is a Frogger! Roger is a Frogger!" then, "We got the herring! We got the herring!"

Eventually, the hands pulled away, and the chants receded to the other parts of the house. No longer contained to the den, the children could be heard in the bathrooms, in the attic, and jumping up and down on Roger and Tamera's bed. If any children were left in the kitchen, they didn't bother Roger as he crawled on hands and knees to the hallway and out the front door. Once outside, he took the extra measure of climbing to the roof via the trellis put up by Tamera one Sunday last Spring.

"Come on up," Tamera said, motioning for him with a slim, sweeping hand. She was already on the roof, perched on one of the severer slopes. Her hair looked freshly washed and blew slightly to the west. "I'm trying to find our house," she said, looking out towards the horizon. "I figured I could see it from up here."

Roger stepped off the trellis onto the roof. Immediately, he felt the reality of the pitch and went back to all fours. He crawled up next to his wife, gingerly turned towards the horizon, and chose a position half sitting and half lying, splaying his legs at what he believed to be a safe angle despite the fact that he was in his robe.

"I thought next Sunday we could go out of town," Tamera said. "Maybe take the kids to the lake. But you'll have to get up early, you know."

Roger nodded and ventured a glance over the rooftops. In the distance, he thought he saw his house, their house, and on the roof, himself and Tamera staring back at him. He dug his heels into the shingles so deep that tiny pieces of asphalt skipped off the roof. He never heard them hit the ground.

Bottles

Robert Hibbard

*P*arsons drank the rest of the screwdriver, then set
the Charlie Chaplin glass near the phone. He
licked orange pulp off his lower lip as he checked
the TV screen again, then slapped the side of the
Magnavox so hard he wondered if he hadn't done it this
time, hadn't broken his hand on some piece of junk. He
rubbed his palm on his jeans, hunched over and tried
the rabbit ears again.

The TV was from a garage sale the week before, a
"goddamn bargain" the white-haired woman who sold it
to him had said. He'd nodded. There was a smell of
whiskey. Parsons wondered if she was drunk, too.

"I'll throw the rabbit ears and the remote in for free,"
she'd bellowed. He'd forced a laugh and said okay, but
looked away as soon as she started peeling the price off
the set. His eyes shifted back and forth between *Leave it
to Beaver* on the TV and his car parked on the curb.

He told himself he should have known he was being
taken. He gave the TV another smack. Still nothing but
silence and static. He made a fist and thought about
shards of black plastic exploding in all directions,
embedding themselves into his hand, or maybe into the
walls, he thought, or the bookshelf.

The digital clock said eight. Parsons's wife would wake
up in an hour and get ready to work the night shift. He
straightened his back and gave the set a few quiet taps.
Nothing. He took his glass and went into the kitchen, on
the way ramming his hand into the empty vodka bottle
jutting out of the trash. "Ow," he whispered.

Parsons wrote her a note on the back of an envelope
and left it near the stack of bills he'd pulled it from.
"Took twenty for vodka," the note said. "Night's lonely

without you. Back in a bit." He sandwiched the bill between the ten and the liquor store receipt still in his wallet from earlier and headed out the door.

A couple of kids were playing with a beer bottle in front of the apartment laundromat. Parsons felt something sting his arm. Gnats and mosquitoes, attracted by the flourescent light glowing through the windows and the heat of the dryers, swarmed in front of the laundromat.

The bigger boy rolled the bottle along the asphalt and said, "Fetch, doggie!" The smaller one, barking, ran into the parking lot after it. He crawled under a Dodge and got the bottle, then, smiling, held it up.

"Now break it!" the older boy shouted. Parsons heard the glass shatter behind him, and a few seconds later the Dodge started. The woman inside the car shouted, "Get in this car! This second!" Parsons hadn't noticed her.

"You just wait 'til we get home," she yelled. Both boys began crying. Parsons quickened his pace, staggering as he rounded the corner and locked onto the liquor store.

Two Hispanic men stood in front of the store. The lanky one craned his head every few seconds, every time a car passed. Parsons shoved his hands into his pockets and slowed himself.

The shorter man wore a mechanic's jacket with "Rich" sewn over the heart. Parsons let his gaze rise to the man's stubbly face and rubbed his own smooth cheeks while trying to make eye contact. He nodded quickly, and the man turned to his taller friend and said something Parsons didn't catch.

"*Pendejo,*" Parsons heard a different, deeper voice say. Both laughed as Parsons twittered his hand along the handle before grabbing it, hoping to get the expected shock of static electricity over with. Nothing happened. He grabbed the handle and jerked the door open. Bells jingled.

Through a mouthful of frozen pie, the clerk mumbled, "How's it goin'?" Then he forked into the pie and turned a page in the *High Times* he was reading.

"How're you?" Parsons said, hoping the clerk didn't notice the quiver in his voice. Parsons went straight for the vodka.

"Anything I can help you find?" the clerk asked.

"I've got it, " Parsons said.

He walked to the counter and set the bottle beside the pie. He gave the clerk the twenty instead of the ten. The cash drawer opened, the clerk dipped his stubby, half-cupped fingers into the change and handed Parsons thirteen cents. Parsons got a jolt of static electricity. He jerked his arm back.

"Dry as a bone this summer, ain't it?" the clerk said. Parsons looked up at him. The clerk's T-shirt had a Confederate flag iron-on. The clerk shook his head and laughed as the cash drawer slid shut.

"You got you a little somethin' tonight?" he said.

Parsons kept quiet. The clerk licked his lips and ran his eyes over the fork in his hand. Parsons lingered at the register. The clerk gobbled two more pieces of pie.

"Somethin' else I can do you for?" the clerk said. He scooted the pie aside.

"I gave you a twenty," Parsons said. The clerk wrinkled his brow. "Twenty dollars," Parsons repeated. "That was twenty dollars I gave you," he said, again eyeing the change in his hand. "It wasn't ten."

"Nope. Don't believe so."

"No, really," Parsons said, and forced a chuckle. "That was a—"

"You gave me a ten, I gave you your change."

Parsons stared at the bottle and waited, his eyes drawing a bead on the clerk's forehead. His knees were liquid. The clerk raised the last piece of pie to his mouth.

"All I wanna do is finish my dinner," he said. He chewed the pie with his mouth open, swallowed it, and looked Parsons in the eye. Then he burped.

He sat the fork in the empty tin and leaned toward Parsons.

"Don't do this," the clerk warned. He reached under the counter. Parsons heard a heavy thud underneath. "What you wanna do," the clerk said, "is take your bottle and go."

Parsons looked around the clerk's fat neck and saw both of their reflections in the window.

"A bag," Parsons said. He smiled. "I need a bag."

"Hmm?"

Parsons said, "I need a bag to carry this around. You can't carry something like this around—you know, in plain view."

The clerk licked his fork, smacked his tongue and threw the empty pie tin away. He smirked at Parsons.

Parsons grabbed the bottle and pointed it at the clerk. The clerk bagged the bottle and muttered something about Parsons being a pain in the ass.

On his way out, Parsons slammed the door hard enough to crack the glass. The wild jangle of the bells drowned out the clerk's shouting. Parsons ran the five blocks home.

Parsons's wife was in her robe, reclining on the couch and watching TV when he got back. She asked him if he made it okay.

"How the hell'd you get that thing to work?" he asked. She told him it was on when she got up. Parsons said that there was nothing but static when he left, not even a noise.

"Just leave it on for a while," she said. "The picture comes together."

He set the bag down on the counter and rinsed the

dried orange pulp from the glass he'd used earlier. He poured himself the rest of the juice, then opened the vodka and filled the glass the rest of the way.

"You want one?" he asked. She shook her head.

Parsons stirred the drink with his finger. He seated himself on the rug beside the couch. He took a drink, then raised the glass to his wife's mouth. She shook her head. He cradled the drink between his thighs, then raised the finger to her mouth. "Don't," she said.

As she got up to change for work, he reached out to caress her leg and missed. She walked to the bedroom. He muted the TV, waited for her to say something. A dresser drawer was opened and then slammed shut. Hangers clanged. He set the drink on the rug, got up and walked to the table her purse was on and put the ten dollars he had left into her purse. The note was in the same place he'd left it. He wadded it up and hid it under the empty bottle in the trash.

His wife rushed out of the bedroom. She stared straight ahead until she got to the door, then turned. He looked at her.

"I'll be late home tomorrow," she said. He told her that he wished she could call in sick this once. She rummaged through her purse.

"Ooh," she cooed. "Is little he lonesome?"

Parsons looked away. His wife left.

He watched through the blinds as she started the car. She lit a cigarette, a tiny point of light in the darkness, and cracked the window. He wondered when she'd started smoking. She backed out of their parking place.

The remote was sticky. He wiped it on his shirt and sat on the couch. He pressed a button on the remote, and the TV went off. He'd meant to unmute it. Parsons tried everything he could, but it wouldn't come back on.

Hamlet in Texas

Christopher Forrest Givan

On Thursday I drove to Fort Worth which is about two hundred and fifty miles from Oklahoma City. During the rainstorm I listened to all four cassettes of *Hamlet*. I was putting them into the radio/cassette player with one hand so I couldn't get them in order. It didn't matter. Hamlet killed the king in the second cassette and the ghost appeared for the first time as I got off the freeway and began to look for the Hyatt Regency in Fort Worth. The South Central Modern Language Association, fondly known as Scumla, was holding its annual meeting there and I was scheduled to read a fifteen minute paper on "Play Spaces in *Hamlet*," in The Renaissance Drama section, which did not meet until Friday. The three nights in the hotel should be restful since my department was picking up the tab and I didn't have anything to do besides read the paper on Friday morning and then go to other sessions the next two and a half days.

I pulled into the front of the hotel and a young guy in a red suit asked me if I wanted Valet Parking. I declined but arranged that I could leave the car there while I checked in, provided I give him the car key. At the desk I was thrown off balance by seeing a registration clerk in a nun's outfit. I assumed she was a nun supporting her order by working in a hotel. It was upsetting to see her in her black hood and white trim and to have to think about nuns.

A very pale Japanese woman about twenty-seven with straight black hair handled the check-in procedure. I asked if I could have a room with a great view. She checked my registration status and this gave me a chance to imagine wanting to have a relationship with her. She returned to face me across the desk in a pleasant manner and explained that at the conference rate the highest I could be would be a room on the fourth floor. She handed me the key to 412, and I carried my own bags to the golden elevator and stepped in and pushed four.

The two men in the elevator looked like successful executives close to retirement who were meeting in the hotel to discuss their millions. With their brown suits and large noses, they both looked like Iacocca, maybe getting ready for another TV broadcast to pitch Chrysler's new line of cars. I felt hostile. They were older men, with shocks of white hair looking like Yeats or my father, who is retired and lives with my mother in Virginia.

One of the older executives said, "Hey, we are going up again. We are going nowhere fast."

Conscious of wearing jeans, a good sports jacket, and a blue and white summer cap, I said, "You must be Republicans, if you think you are going nowhere."

"What?" said the taller of the two older men, astonished at my rudeness.

"Going nowhere, that is where Bush is taking the country."

"How can you say that?" said the other executive.

"Bush is ignoring domestic problems. He thinks he is king of the world."

"Well, he is," said the other Iacocca and I remembered I was in Texas, probably Bush country through and through.

I got off at the fourth floor and let myself into room 412. It smelled of fresh toothpaste and mouthwash. I rather liked the smell though it was strange. Maybe that is the way they do things in Texas hotels; they clean them with toothpaste or a cleaning agent that smells like mouthwash. Then I noticed the suitcases everywhere. I glanced at the open closet near the door and saw clothes hanging up. I picked up the phone and asked for the desk.

"Hey," I said, "This is Dr. Domo, I am in room 412, the room you just gave me, and it is already occupied. There are suitcases in it."

There was a pause, "You want another room, sir?"

I had an odd moment which reminded me of the time my second wife planned a surprise birthday party when I turned forty, and I was so sorry I had found out about it ahead of time. Later on, she had an affair with my best friend and that was truly a surprise. I hated being betrayed, of course, but in some way, which I don't think shows some secret homoerotic tendencies, I liked it that she had slept with Frank and that the two of them surprised me. (They phoned me up one night when I was at a Shakespeare conference in Massachusetts to tell me they were going to get married. They didn't, of course, as Kathy, Frank's wife, insisted he return to her.)

I paused in room 412 looking again at the array of clothes in the closet and on the bed and wondering if through some larger scheme, I was intended to, in fact, be assigned a new partner and the partner had already checked into the room.

The desk clerk said again, "So, do you want another room, is that it?"

I felt the mantle of indignation fall easily on my shoulders, "Well, only after I finish going through the suitcases and taking what I need. Of course I want another room."

"Who checked you in?"

"It wasn't the nun. It was the Japanese person next to the nun."

"O.K., if you come back down to the desk we will give you another room."

"I want it to have a good view, high up above the city

this time, or I'm going to the manager about this mistake."

There was a pause, and I wondered if I would have gotten better results if I had actually saved the threat about going to the manager for later on.

"Ah, sir," there was a definite change in the person's voice. He had slipped into self-righteous seriousness, "Ah, sir, there is a message here for you. A long distance phone call, an emergency."

I peered around me at the suitcases sitting like abandoned relics of another era. The toothpaste smell seemed stronger, more medicinal.

"Yeah, what is the message?"

"There has been a death in your family, sir, I am very sorry."

"You must have the wrong person."

"No, you should come down to the registration desk, sir, I think so."

His speech patterns now made me think it was the Hispanic man that was standing next to the Japanese woman when I checked in.

"Who is dead in my family?" I waited for a reply thinking that maybe just as I had been given the wrong room, a room already occupied, maybe this message was for the occupants of room 412, not me.

The line purred a dial tone. I would have to take the elevator back down with my two briefcases and duffel bag to find out who was dead in my family. I prayed it was a mistake. I pushed the elevator button. My dad? My mom? The driving rain on the freeway for four hours from Oklahoma had seemed to pour its blinding greyness over me, and I could hear Hamlet intoning on and on, about the marriage tables and the funeral meats and the ghost summarizing the action at the end since I had gotten the cassettes out of order. Those bastards at the registration desk must have the wrong person.

I clambered onto the first elevator that opened on the fourth floor and found myself going up instead of down. The nun from the front desk was already in the elevator. She wore a bright magenta shade of lipstick highly evident as she also wore her black habit and white headpiece across the top of her brown hair. I felt myself growing warm, insane, worried about which of my parents was dead.

I said to the nun, "Did you get a message at the desk just now for Flaven Domo, for me, saying that one of my parents is dead?"

She looked at me and said, "I am not a real nun. This is a Halloween costume."

I didn't say anything. I felt betrayed. I had not respected her as a nun. I am certainly not a Catholic, though my second wife was, but I felt something had been taken away from me that she wasn't a real nun. Maybe in that ghastly moment of stress wondering which of my parents was gone forever, I wanted to be near a nun. I wanted her to be the bearer of this terrible news. A baby sitter once when I was eight gave me very clear directions on how to behave if you see a ghost. I have never forgotten them.

The nun said, "It is the thirty-first of October, Halloween, that is why I am in costume."

She got out on the tenth floor. The elevator with its own robotic hum climbed up the fourteenth floor. For no reason at all I got out.

The doors closed behind me. The corridor was empty and looked like a hallway on the Titanic. The carefully vacuumed grey and red carpet, which had flower patterns in it like a mosaic I remembered seeing once with my parents in Ravenna, seemed now to be part of a museum that had once served bygone emperors or now defunct citizens. The long corridor with its evenly spaced doorways, each with a small door handle protruding like a truncated appendage, seemed so still and empty.

I wondered why I had not prepared for this moment, prepared for my parents' death, prepared for at least one of their deaths. I wondered which one of them was dead.

I pushed the elevator button. Which parent did I want to be dead? I have always gotten along with them separately better than when they were a team together. They had been married fifty years last summer. My mother, in a way, might be easier to entertain and deal with, care for, than my Dad, if she were the one who was left, but she had never fully recovered from her parents' deaths which occurred when she was still a child. And she had gotten somewhat unpredictable lately, taking her retirement from teaching a bit hard, whereas my father was more mellow, having developed a love of his computer and other hobbies so that his retirement was, perhaps, easier for him.

My years with them didn't end when I went to college at eighteen, but through my three marriages I seemed to have carried my parents with me. I carried my parents with me the way Queequeg in *Moby Dick* carried his little god with him in a bag that he took out and worshipped each night and then would toss the wooden ikon back into his duffel bag.

The first wife, married at twenty-one, accepted that we would commute between my parents and hers at all vacations and take our place in some kind of ritual at Thanksgiving and Christmas and so forth. My father gave me a special wrench for household tasks when I married the first time. The second wife had been Romanian and we lived in Europe and so I didn't see too much of my parents though they gave us a vacuum cleaner which worked fine during the six months we tried Stateside jobs. It wouldn't work when we moved to Switzerland.

The third wife was from New Hampshire, and she wouldn't even talk to me about my unresolved relationship to my father or my concern about my mother. She divorced me after three years and took both horses, much to my relief.

The elevator deposited me in the lobby. I always rose to the occasion. I was good in a crisis. It would mean calling my sisters who now both lived in Europe. I would need to be the one who made the funeral arrangements. I hoped I would be able to give my *Hamlet* paper tomorrow morning and then fly out. Writing this paper had been the only scholarship I had done in five years. It represented a return to giving papers and maybe a return to writing the Shakespeare book. One of my parents dying should not undermine my giving the *Hamlet* paper.

I walked across the lobby, my two briefcases and dirty white duffel bag banging against my legs and hips as if I were crippled and couldn't walk normally. Then, I saw Tom Reilly, whom I had not seen for six years; that was two jobs ago for me. He looked older and fatter, puffed up like a sausage, his skin stretched across his face in middle-aged contentment. He saw me and came over to say hello. His first words were, "I got promoted and tenured last year and I bought the house I was renting."

I put down my duffel and shook his hand, "How is your cat?" I asked, hoping his cat was dead.

"Shelia is fine," he said, and I remembered now thinking that he was gay back when we both taught in New Mexico. Tom added, "I'm chairing the Muriel Spark section. Incidentally, is Alexandra doing okay these days?"

Alexandra was the name of my blue-eyed Romanian wife who had had the affair with Frank, Tom Reilly's office mate.

"Alexandra is fine. She became a therapist and works in Chicago."

Reilly lit a cigarette as if he were in a Clint Eastwood western, very slow and poised. I decided again that he was most likely gay. I felt like asking him about this, but decided I wanted to end what I hoped would be our one encounter per decade on a neutral note.

"Did you ever get your own office?" I asked.

He was telling me how the Dean had gotten everyone a terrific office with a view of the eastern New Mexico high plains, when I noticed that one of the clerks, the Japanese woman with the lovely crescent-shaped eyes, was beckoning me to the desk.

"Professor Domo," she said in a pleasant nourishing maybe flirtatious tone, "I am sorry you were given the wrong room. We have found a room for you on the fourteenth floor with a view of the city, of the train track and the famous stock yards."

"Great," I said, putting the duffel bag down and wishing she could be my fourth wife as long as I could get through this day all right.

"Listen," I said, "Is there a message for me? Something about a death in my family?"

Her almond eyes looked at me and then looked away. "I will check." She looked at a level of the desk that was hidden from the customer and then looked behind her at the pigeonholes where they put messages.

"I'm sorry, Professor Domo, no messages for you."

"But I was told on the phone when I was in room 412 that there was a message, that someone had died in my family."

The Japanese woman now reminded me of the Polynesian woman in *South Pacific*, who has the love affair with the American pilot who later dies but not before he sings "Are You Younger Than Spring Time?" My Japanese clerk moved delicately down the desk and conferred with the Hispanic man about the message. He said something to her and she returned to me.

"Professor Domo, there was a message about a death but it was not for you, it was for someone else."

I felt relief and anger and gratitude at the inefficiency of the Hyatt Regency in Fort Worth. This would never happen in Dallas. Dallas was oil money, whereas Fort Worth was cattle. They were country bumpkins here. They couldn't deliver a message about death if their lives depended on it.

The Japanese woman looked at me, her smooth white skin so lovely with her dark straight hair cut in bangs over her white forehead. Would she marry me?

"So there is no message?" I said, "and no one is dead?"

"No message for you, the death is not connected to you."

I felt so happy. I knew I would have to call my parents and verify their being alive. I would be able to read my *Hamlet* paper after all. I would be able to postpone taking my father to dinner after my mother is dead, postpone playing Hearts with my mother after my father is dead and watching TV with her. Of course, I might die before they die.

I accepted from that lovely delicate white hand, which could be moving a long brush over a smooth parchment making purple and black characters, the key to 1410. I turned once more to drag my burdens across the lobby to the golden elevators. In my confusion I dropped the duffel bag and felt the ikons bumping against each other, or to be more exact the bottle of Jack Daniels and the jar of Planters Peanuts I had smuggled in. I wondered for an instant if there is an afterlife and if perhaps it involves living for an indeterminate amount of time in a large hotel in Fort Worth where you don't make love, you don't even get drunk, but you just float from academic session to academic session, ricocheting from AMLit before 1800 to Flaubert and Conrad and bouncing off of Semiotics and Christianity and Literature without ever coming to rest.

When I called my parents, I got their recording and I assumed they were out at their favorite Chinese restaurant made more famous because President Bush dines there too, with the Secret Service of course.

Feeling oddly as if I had been told that I didn't have cancer, I phoned the desk while looking at the night skyline of Fort Worth. Beyond the stock yards were old rusting trains and there in the huge picture frame came a functioning train lapping up the miles. The Japanese woman answered.

I said, "I'm Professor Domo, you just gave me the key to room 1410. I am here to give a Shakespeare paper," I paused.

She said, "Really. I am a graduate student at Denton, in English. Maybe I will come hear it."

I wanted to ask her if her parents had both been killed in Hiroshima. I then felt afraid that she was related somehow to one of the Iacoccas in the elevator.

"What is your name?"

"Ayako Arakawa," she said. I could hear another phone ringing beside her.

"Listen, Ayako, would you like to have dinner with me tonight?"

She accepted and I hung up. I wanted to run down all fourteen flights and be glad of something. I wanted, maybe, to see the rich businessman types again and apologize, but I hadn't been that rude after all. I knew for some reason that I would have a love affair with Ayako, or at least a short love affair and it would be all right. Only I wouldn't count on that; oh no. I would be very modern and count only on the dinner and the talk of Shakespeare and her graduate work. The phone rang again. It was Ayako. She said she couldn't have dinner after all, she had to replace someone at the desk. My heart fell. It was absurd to go through this again, to even vaguely imagine in this cow town that there could be the kind of unexpected romance or encounter that I used to have anywhere in the world.

"Tomorrow," she said, sounding like *The Tale of Genji,* "after your Shakespeare paper, we could have lunch, okay?"

I told Ayako that lunch would be fine, located my small bottle of whiskey, opened the peanuts, and lying back in that huge empty emperor-sized bed, turned on the evening news.

Archangelsk

Jim Drummond

"There is the noted swing," Vera said. George Segal had sat in it while Richard Burton probed him for split seams, in *Who's Afraid of Virginia Woolf?* Vera's "House" at Smith served as the exterior of George and Martha's house in this scene. I tried the swing.

"Well!" I said. "Shall we not sit there together?"

As when, bearing down with one's arms on the rotary crank of a tennis net, one succeeds in pushing the sharp lip of the gear over the next tooth of its sprocket, then lets it fall back into its disciplined straight tension, then so we, after a series of crescive correspondences by mail, slipped down a notch in the tenor of our anticipations, realizing perhaps in the same faint instant—our first view of one another in the parlor of the "House" where I'd come to collect her—that neither smoke nor voltage would attend our acquaintance.

She smiled to show she knew I was kidding about sitting in the swing where George and Richard sat, which I was not. I wanted something pleasant, and if I couldn't get that, something with bite. "Sure?" I asked. "After all, in the movie, Richard had George's name. Would you like me as Vera?"

It might have been promising. (I could hardly get more conditional—more playing-it-safe.) Rex Yellerman, my associate editor on the *Cyclops,* had prattled with bombast over Vera, who was the most beautiful, simple, brilliant, supple, scintillating woman he had ever known, seen, or heard rumored. VERA DUMPS SIX FEET OF SNOW ON SCORELESS REX, read Rex's headline. (Last year he was Sports and Weather.)

Well, it turned out I'd met her. She'd been down to the college for a party weekend three years earlier; I didn't meet many girls so I remembered most of them. She had been propped on Chad Lodrescu's dorm bed, chording a guitar and singing, her leg in a full cast (skiing). "She's an angel," I'd thought, sneaking my looks on fake runs to the water fountain, captivated with her black glossy hair in lush pigtails. Now it was straight, and she had grown taller and leaner. (Two years in a Geneva university had intervened.)

So over several weeks I wrote her a serialized Joyce spoof about the shark as the retributive agent against lapsed Catholics, called *Sin Again, Fin Again.* Headlines were not the path to an audience with Vera. Being positioned at the right angle to catch the glint of the mica, that is, being informed as to the *esoteric context* of the pertinent allusion or *bon mot*, worked with her. "No dance, no chance, little Boy." When I say, "worked with her," I mean, it elicited sparkling laughs of higher estimation—no more.

Which was silly but a fair flag of those sixties days when most varsity minds were spermatozoa, nearsighted (salmon?) swimmers. You certainly couldn't rely on your senses or sensations, much less on ordinary courtship procedures, tentative small talking. Which was fine with me, the original Mr. Weirdwit.

Friday of Fall House Parties I picked her up in Northampton. In the front seat of my cardinal-colored Firebird, Vera turned her eyes on me with a snowy smile and told me with jewel-cutter precision that I held no sexual interest for her.

"Is it the hollow look in my eyes?" I cried. "Or the livery of my lips?"

"Oh, no, you have a good-natured face. Rather, it's chemistry; we've no electrons to trade."

"You mean, 'It's *phys*ics.'" She laughed.

"Your letter was wonderfully funny. I loved the Russian fisherman."

"The Snorkel of Arkhangelsk," I corrected. A prophet of my invention who'd swum from Finland with sardines for the icebound peasants who were starving because of a raid of seven thousand whale-riding Inuits, which depleted their stores. Hardly a mere quaint fisherman, but that was her tone. I was miffed; if it was so memorable, if it penetrated, would she so airily err?

🪶　🪶　🪶　🪶　🪶

At the College, we went straight to Guild House: this passed for a Student Union. Varnished oak tables with Lazy Susans were carved with a century of complacent nihilist names. Wall lamps issued brown light.

Vera talked vividly, in long stretches, often designating things and laughing at points foreign to my erudition. She laughed, narrowly as a tensor lamp, upon quoting Picasso's alleged remark that he was "hideously constrained to appease the penumbra." Her crisp inhalations, the broad slender smile which tore her lovely face like a California snow-fig and hid her deep-ridged eyes, covered me with neutrons and remote distance. I found myself nearly bored with her conversation, yet uncomfortably magnetized. I imagine exiles like Dreyfus, le Papillon, and Napoleon on their islands felt the same about fickle France's miserable mystery.

Edward Crips appeared, rich reddish hair parted in the middle to crest at each side and crash down the beach of his psychological temples (now I would just say he was a redheaded psych major)—he was the closest thing to a friend I had, and I made introductions. He and I were both reticent in the teeth of her presence, which was so mothily schizoid, as one of Crips's poems might drone, so snowflakily prismatic. Vera talked so fast that I had no chance to bring Crips in. In a few minutes he left

25

wordlessly, incensed; Vera did not blink if she noticed. I almost envied Crips the clarity of his impression and position with respect to Vera. With her mind racing to keep ahead of my touch or my sex or my mere flesh, this Atalanta hardly noticed *me*, it appeared.

I wanted her warmth, so nimbly withheld from me, almost as a car with half-full tank might want gas, *de rigueur*, from some mechanical convention. Yet her touch did not stir me up, nor scratch any itch; it was always light, a mime of affection and animation. It made me snowblind.

"Where am I staying?" The inflection rose up purely on the last word in a lace-veil of courtesy. ("It will most certainly not be in the same room with your *flesh*," said the Queen to Mr. Weird.) At last I could not restrain my inner lyric:

"Where stay? In the well of my arms, in my heart's bucket, Juliana:

> Tell me where I may pass the fires
> Of the hot day, or hot desires.
> To what cool cave shall I descend,
> Or to what gelid fountain bend?"

I didn't actually say that. I didn't wish I'd said that.

The best I could do for her was a spare bed in the garret of the Halfway House, which some friends operated for out-patients; I stayed there more than in my own apartment. On the stairs we passed one of the residents, a fellow named Gus with a large gut. Gus was carrying a beer, and wearing a flannel shirt and jean cutoffs, displaying a footlong surgical scar on his right leg. In fact he was a jazz clarinetist of some recording fame, which of course Vera could not know. The bed I'd cadged her was really a cot, with old white sheets from the laundry service and a navy blanket.

"I know! Let's go to New York!" Vera exclaimed.

Her grandparents lived there, far from this squalor.

We went for a drink in midtown New York, night coming early; then we waltzed around the Numbered Streets for an hour, singing spirituals: "Rockababy Jesus," "Devil Up a Stump," "When the Roll Is Called Up Yonder, I'll Be There," "The Burning Bush," "The Imp in the Bottle." We both knew a bunch of them. Vera grew slightly warmer in New York, more faceted yet of softer elements, like a jello diamond. I tried to thaw at these less low temperatures. A touch of her sweater now and then, or walking instantly into the rhythmic vapor of our breath. But it was scant, definitely scant.

After I deposited her at 10:30, just late enough for me not to be insulted, I wandered down Park Avenue to 51st, then over and down to Times Square. A bench was free, one I'd sat on all night with no place to sleep last weekend when Crips and I had hitched to New York to listen to jazz at Slug's (our sage savvy employed to decide who was playing on smack), then search for little matchboxes of cannabis in Washington Square.

I sat down, lit a smoke. A plump black man approached, fairly well-dressed.

"Want to make $50?"

"Who wouldn't?" I said toughly. Few could have had less need for $50; I was well-heeled. But I found art in the idea of posturing as poor. "Doing what?" I added, sarcastically.

"Oh, how wise you are to ask, how wise. A shrewd man, careful of pitfalls. All you must do is to allow me to photograph you having naked sex with a beautiful 21-year old Italian girl, who is in a nearby hotel."

"You are beautiful, but hardly 21, Italian, female," I retort.

"I am leveling. Here is her picture." I almost believe him now, because in fact she is not particularly beautiful, though not ugly either.

"No," I say, "despite what must be your prodigious camera skills, I do not believe this could be your self-portrait."

"This is a business proposition. The question is not my sex but your sex."

"I'm male."

"Are you sure? Lawrence Durrell notes that there are nine genders in Alexandria."

"Woooh!" I exclaim. "These pictures you'll take clearly aren't for *Naked Model Gazette,* they're for *Yellow Silk.* The one Henry Miller reads. Well. Lead on."

I was scared, but I was doing it for Vera. She really pissed me off.

The picture of the girl, the pictures of me, the greenback picture of U.S. Grant—they all turned out to be real. I made him swear the magazine would supply today's date with the photo credit or caption. They did; I sent it to her five months later with the date underlined in red. She told Rex about it: who the hell was that? Whose birthday card missent? Happy belated birthday.

🐁　🐁　🐁　🐁　🐁

Sunday morning I called at her grandparents' apartment on Park Avenue. I forgot the name Vera had given me until the congenial doorman was checking with the grandmother on the phone—then it shot out of me—"Klerck!"—and I was in. I sat on their couch, setting my overcoat beside me. "Put it in the closet, please," said Mrs. Klerck with a hard, discourteous smile. There is an iron vigor and then again a blood vigor of old age; they spring from different pools entirely, similar to the co-evolutionary Arizona cactus and South African euphorbia.

"No thank you!" I said cheerfully, as if declining a drink. La Klerck sucked in her breath, but what could she say?

"Let me take you away from this!" I exhorted Vera as she emerged, a dreamy collage of muffs—ears, hands, sleeves, collar. Sauterne occurred to me—at a table on the floor of the ice rink, its ice freshly brushed, a red rose on the table with shad roe and New Orleans beignets in drifts of powdered sugar. Perhaps a Flying Fish head in the center on an ironstone platter. No skate tracks away from the table. Our waiter must be an angel, a Throne or maybe a Power, at least.

Vera in her muffs took apparel language beyond body language the way Haagen Dazs took ice cream beyond Neapolitan. I was stunned.

I drove Vera down to the East Village looking for a place to eat breakfast. She had her eye on a Russian bakery we could not find—herself being Muscovitish—so we took croissants and coffee in a lunch counter next to a Ukrainian church. Vera was stubborn about not having a full breakfast.

Church let out, the café filled. Awnee govoryat po-russkiy. (Russian spoken here.) I listened to it, borscht-Russian in contrast to the pure vodka of bass orthodox incantations just piously concluded in the cathedral. In contrast as well to the film of grape juice on the wafer of communion with Vera.

🖎 🖎 🖎 🖎 🖎

Christmas vacation we drove in my Firebird to Chicago—two others, Glen and Karen. There was heavy snow through Buffalo and East Ohio. Vera and I were sleeping among piled suitcases in the back seat of my car.

"Feel free to use my shoulder," Vera had said airily. "Likewise," I replied. "But not at the same time, preferably."

Later while I drove she put her arms around my neck from behind, theatrically pretended to be mad about me. This was kind fondness, and I should be grateful.

She was really mad for a sociologist with whom she'd co-produced a film, Rick Berry, it appeared. (She'd tried everything to dislodge my icicle from her eaves and now it was this show of heat for another.) When I was departing Chicago in my Firebird for Oklahoma, she kissed me neutrally on the cheeks, and called me her "Swiss." I groaned methodically, with some conjured stony desire, tired of denial, buried deep in earth. "Is that how they did it in Geneva?" I asked.

"You fool," she trilled, kissing me more carefully. "I've been crazy for you from the beginning. That out-Joycing of Joyce. Those spiritual songs. Cornholing Grammy Klerck right where she lived! And now leaving, irresistibly *leaving*—for Oklahoma . . . You want to be loved, not love? Great! I love Plato! Let's go get some *hamburger*!"

Honorable Discharge

Jim Drummond

Well, I guess they had it backwards. When I was four, Jesus came upon a wild hog, who was rooting our crops in the gardens in the town where I grew up. Abner Hymn was the best gardener around, unwittingly friends with the divas of fragrance and color, and his patch suffered the worst depredations; it was a mean hog with good taste. Abner complained loudly to Jesus. Jesus saw a woman who was shushing a crying baby, and Jesus winced, then said to the demon in the hog: get into that baby. And the demon jumped out of the hog and into the baby. And both the hog and the baby shut up. The woman was my mother.

🐗   🐗   🐗   🐗   🐗

Finding your real home, they say, is very tranquilizing. But that's apocryphal. Demons, mosquitoes, earwigs and moles are never supposed to wonder where they belong. This unanswered question is not seen as the root of their behaviors. Animals have no place they own. It's not theirs by right.

🐗   🐗   🐗   🐗   🐗

Big Jeff was my father. This name was mysterious, but he'd come home with his army friends calling him that, and it stuck. Usually someone comes home from the army alone and scarred, or alone and buoyant, or alone and mean, or alone and neurotic, or alone and silent, or alone and loud. But Big Jeff didn't come home alone at all. He came home with Black Beggs and Red Garwin, and he kept around them. When Garwin bought land, Big Jeff went to work for him, and so did Beggs. And this land was mostly for cattle. Winter wheat and hay were all for the Hereford cattle. Garwin called it the Hard Red Ranch, and he meant that for a lot of things: the baldfaced red cattle; red skin, natural for Garwin and burnt for Big Jeff; the winter wheat variety, which could grow in red clay with five inches of annual rain and could make your muscles flush when you cooked it, it was so full of niacin. (It was a secret Comanche strain, its kernels kept hidden by Comanche brujas who worked in quarries and drove school activity buses.)

〽   〽   〽   〽   〽

There was a long time of princely uncertainty. Though Jeff said the baby barely looked better than a slew of mangy old hogs he'd repossessed that day. What else could it have been, since they stuck nitrate drops in his eyes so they swelled into encased green walnuts, pinching the little face red with pain. Mom's determinedly standard smile; yes the cold rooms were normal, the eyedrops, the circumcision, the separation, the formula, the litany of infantile complaints visible as evidentiary lead pellets in some future new age tribunal. But every one was true, and real, and what could Mom do to mute her inside screams but smile the expected smile you'd smile at an alien or at the black conqueror who'd just successfully captured your suburb from the Alabama National Guard and who was the son of Emperor Jones and Tina Turner? The hardest horror, the one that is seldom faced, is the horror of what you've let someone do to your charge.

The Trip

Laura Holcomb McNatt

Emmaline woke early, and the nagging tick of the clock, together with the disquieting thought that she had fibbed to Joan, kept her from falling back asleep. She lay in bed thinking about the fib . . . really, just a little white lie, and all for the best.

"You know, mother," Joan had said, "I'd love to drive you to Glenville, but I can't. But promise me you won't drive. You'll ride with one of the others."

"Whatever," Emmaline had said.

"Promise me you won't drive," Joan insisted.

Emmaline had sighed, "Don't worry about it."

I didn't exactly say I wouldn't drive, Emmaline reasoned. Joan shouldn't be borrowing trouble. I'm perfectly capable of driving. We will be back before dark. It's my turn to drive. Besides, how would Joan know? She's in Ringgold, thirty-five miles away.

In the four years she had been a widow, Joan and Edward had been the best children a mother could hope for. They did so much for her. Really, too much. They had their own families to worry about. And now that Joan, bless her heart, had been left alone with so much responsibility, why should she do everything for me? Sometimes, she thought, I feel smothered.

She eased to the edge of the bed and sat for a minute to steady herself and loosen the kinks before getting up. It was 5:10 a.m., very dark outside, but when she snapped the kitchen light on, the outdoors came alive. Gray and Stripe clawed at the screen door, and Packard lazily lifted his head as if to inquire if all was well. She wrapped her robe around her and stepped out in the chill of the early November morning to put food out for the strays that had put their roots down in her yard. "You all act like it's seven o'clock."

While the coffee was perking, she sat at the piano and played her basic warm-up chords in the key of C, then swept into "Indian Love Call," which was too high to sing, and wound up singing a few bars of "Oh give me land, ta da da, don't fence me in."

At 6:30, she ran a comb through her smoke-gray hair that would be snow-white if she could resign herself to the fact that at age seventy-nine some people do have white hair. She rouged her lips and stepped into her shoes. She knew that across town, Muriel would be getting ready. From their many years of friendship, and the occasional overnight trips they took, she could follow Muriel's routine. She would be standing before the mirror, all made up, with little curls she had unwound before bedtime still intact. Her head would look like a new-mown field with coppery-gray bales neatly rolled hear and there. White scalp pathways would weave between the curls, and she would flatten them with a neatly coiffured, copper-brown wig.

Muriel was three years younger than Emmaline, smaller and more delicate. She had a soft voice, and even softer eyes, brown like a cocker pup, and magnified by thick lenses she had worn since childhood. Her delicate air was deceiving. She had the constitution of a combat marine.

At five minutes until seven, Emmaline locked the back door, and, seeing the morning paper had finally arrived, picked it up and tossed it, along with a sweater, in the back seat. Five minutes later, she gave a *toot toot* on the horn, and Muriel slid in the passenger seat. "Isn't it a lovely morning?"

"Just perfect for a trip," Emmaline said. Who needed a chauffeur?

As they zoomed west down the highway, sometimes

hitting forty-five miles an hour, the winter sun rolled higher in the sky, not hot like a summer sun, but further away and smaller, warming the car to a comfortable degree. The grass, now a yellowish tan, was sparkling with dew that would burn off as the morning wore on.

This was a day of freedom. There was no one hovering over them, telling them what they could, or couldn't do. No one hinting that they should stay home where they belong. They would not burden themselves with talk of the district club meeting they were going to in Glenville. They spoke of their contemporaries. "Poor May," said Muriel, "she's going to wither if she doesn't get out of that chair and quit acting so helpless. How does she expect to be independent if she won't help herself? She doesn't eat enough to keep a mite alive."

"I know," sighed Emmaline. "She should be more like Fred Wilson. He had a pain the other day and Josie called the ambulance and he got his hat and rode up front with the driver. Speaking of independence! And you know what happened when Barbara Ann took John's keys away. Good-bye freedom!"

"She says they just drive her up the wall."

"Where is *up the wall?*" Emmaline asked. "I went up to see them the other day. It was only six o'clock and Lola had already tucked John in for the night. It's a good thing I stopped by. She had left one arm out of his pajama top and had him buttoned is so that his arm was twisted."

"Oh well, it's a good thing they had a double available at the Manor. Otherwise, what would they have done? I hope," Muriel continued, "I never live to see the day when Aaron and Adam try to put me away. I'll tell them, 'this is my money and you're not touching it!' Of course they wouldn't try."

"Of course not," Emmaline said. "Mine wouldn't either." She felt unrighteous saying anything against Edward or Joan, bless their hearts, but she didn't want to feel intimidated by Muriel, so she added, "I'll tell them, 'this is my bed, and this is where I plan to sleep.'"

They reached the divided highway at Littlefork that was not much more than a '66 station with a few stocked grocery items, with a very small post office in one corner; and the H and L Diner next door. The gas station attendant and his wife, the postmistress, lived in a mobile home out back. In the distance there was a sprinkling of small houses.

The direction arrows at the Y intersection pointed left to Glenville, right to Greenwood. Had Emmaline turned right, as she almost always did, they would have come to Greenwood where Edward owned a pharmacy. This was club day, though, and Emmaline turned left. They sailed through the small towns of Jasper and Mitchell, and on to the First United Methodist Church of Glenville where the district homemakers were to meet.

Emmaline and Muriel found the meeting less than motivating, in fact, dull. They weren't particularly inspired by the session *Crafts for the Elderly,* nor did they like *Better Nutrition in Later Years.* They enjoyed visiting with ladies of neighboring clubs, and the luncheon was lovely. The trip to Glenville had been pleasant, and they looked forward to a genial trip home. They had done their duty by attending, and would report back to the home club.

"I believe we'll have time to stop for a sandwich and still make it home before dark, don't you?" Emmaline asked.

"I should think so. Might even have a beer. Doesn't that sound good?"

"We'll see what we can find," Emmaline answered. "Now you watch the signs."

At Jasper they pulled up to a restaurant where Emmaline thought the sign said *Coors* but really said *Coke.* As they were getting out, the two other cars from home passed by. The ladies honked and waved. "I'm glad they didn't stop," said Muriel. "We would have had to hide our beer behind the ketchup."

Before long they were back on the road. The western sky was a cool yellow-orange. "Now Muriel, watch for the Littlefork turnoff."

"We can't miss it," Muriel replied. Yet somewhere between talk of poor old Mr. Symbob, who is so lonely, and Ethyl wandering into Mrs. Adams' room because *she can't see two feet in front of her anymore,* and Mrs. Adams shouting *get outta here,* they did miss it. They found themselves on the outskirts of Greenwood.

"Oh well," Emmaline said, "we don't have to backtrack. We'll just go on east to Prairietown and drop back down to Littlefork. Just a short detour," she chuckled.

A few minutes later they came to a small town. "What's this?" Muriel asked.

"I think it's Prairietown, but I'm not sure. Why don't you run in that station and ask how we get to Littlefork?"

Muriel came back with directions. "The fastest way is on an unpaved county road, but it's in good shape. We take it for fourteen miles and then turn left on a road that meets the Littlefork highway."

Off they went down the dirt road, twenty-five miles per hour. They didn't bother to count the miles because they knew they were headed in the right direction, and, well, they forgot. They chatted away until Emmaline interrupted the conversation. "Don't you think we've gone about fourteen miles?"

"It seems like it. Why don't we turn left on the next road."

Emmaline turned. The road was bumpy, and she slowed down to keep better control. The sun had dropped below the horizon, and the day moon raced to catch it. They went up and down small hills and inclines for about six miles when they came abruptly to a small canyon. "Oh Muriel, that gorge. I don't believe I can make it."

"Of course you can. I'll get out and direct you." Muriel climbed out, and with arms outstretched, palms up, gave the come-on signal with wiggling fingers. Emmaline eased ahead; then suddenly the sandy soil crumbled the side of the road, and the right front tire slid into a ditch. She tried backing, but the rear wheels spun, digging deeper into the sand.

Off in the distance they could see lights. "I see a farmhouse," Muriel said. "You stay here and I'll go for help. Let me have your shoes." She traded her high-heel sandals for Emmaline's sensible, mid-heel pumps.

Emmaline twisted to ease the aches in her shoulders and stretched her legs to unwind the knotted muscles that cramped them. I knew better than to try to make this, she thought. I should have turned around...or backed up. Muriel should have known better, but that's Muriel; unafraid of a roaring train if she was tied to the tracks. Joan will call to see how the day went, then she will call Muriel—and Pearl, and Irene—to see if they are home yet. Oh, bless her little heart. I'll worry her. *I'll drive her up the wall.*

Muriel started for the lights that looked like little blinking eyes. She scooted in baby steps trying to keep the size eight shoes on her size six feet, and the ragged grass scratched at her legs. She clutched two dollar bills and a quarter in her closed fist, because she thought you never know when you may need a little money.

The sky arched black overhead and the sparse scattering of diamond stars gave little light. The monotony of the rolling pasture was deceiving. It rose and dipped in uneven places, and she stumbled several times when the neglected grass camouflaged pits in the terrain. Dried sod clung to her jacket, and the knuckles on one hand, the palm of the other were stinging from the scratches etched into her flesh. But she continued on toward the lights. As she drew nearer, she realized that they were lights on an oil tank, and upon reaching it, found it unattended. "Lord, what will you have me do," she prayed.

Far in the distance she saw faint lights; Littlefork, she thought. She started toward them. "I wish to heavens *I* had driven today," she said to herself. The night was overwhelmingly silent. Still and dark. She recalled the dust devils that used to swirl out on the farm, but not on this night. Not even the branches of the occasional hackberry swished.

She came to the rim of a ravine and edged along in a circular pattern as if performing a dance she had seen at a Pow Wow. As she fought to keep upright, her foot became tangled in the thick, scruffy underbrush and she lost a shoe. She dropped to her knees and fished around as if blindfolded. When she lost the other, she shrugged, thinking none is as good as one. A barbed wire fence outlined the top of the ravine. She lay flat on her back and scooted under. *Lord, don't let me ruin this new dress. It cost ninety dollars.* Her copper-brown wig snagged on a tumbleweed caught in the fence, but when she tried to retrieve it with one hand, it snagged even worse. She relaxed her fist and felt only the coin. She clutched it and said aloud, "Sometimes money doesn't count—doesn't help. Has no value." She plodded on and within a short time could hear the buzz of trucks on a highway somewhere. But where? Oil rig lights reflected in a creek that she came upon, and she waded in ankle-deep mud, and it felt good on her feet. She rested on the bank and thought of gyppie water and cisterns with rope pulleys. She was so tired.

The clock on the dash beamed nine o'clock. Emmaline's mind alternated between fleeting moments of the past and the reality of the present. She had thought of life on this bluestem prairie; of the pioneers who had come to this land in covered wagons and had lived in dug-outs until their soddies were finished. She had been young when her family came west. Six years old. She used to make her children laugh when she told them her favorite toy was an old stick that she threw across the narrow creek so she could jump after it. Many folk burned cow chips for fuel, but her mother wouldn't. Now there are cow chip throwing contests. I can't imagine anyone getting pleasure from throwing a cow chip! Here I am, right where they gather their ammunition. Other events that had been shadows for years came back to life.

She knew that by now Joan was frantic. She would have called Pearl and Irene and learned that Muriel hadn't driven. She would have called Edward and sent him out to look for them, and she and little David would be slowly driving the route to Glenville, searching for any sign that their car had careened off the road into a ditch. Edward has probably called the sheriff, and only God knows who else, Emmaline thought.

Now, eleven o'clock. She had spent over four nervous hours waiting. Muriel has fallen. Broken a leg. Or hip. She's laying helpless somewhere out there, and I must go for help.

She opened the door and shifted her legs outside so she could take off her hose. The ground was cold on her bare feet. Thank God for mixed blessings, she thought, as she reached for the morning paper that had finally arrived. She shredded part of it and stuffed the soles of her nylons to cushion her feet. She fumbled in her purse for a pen, always cautious now because last year she had been on a trip with Muriel, and in rummaging through her purse she set off the mace gun. Her thumb was healed now, but Muriel doesn't quite let her forget it. She ripped a check from her checkbook, and on the back she wrote, "Muriel, it is 11:00. I'm going for help. Going back the way we came."

The caliche road was rough, but because its whiteness contrasted with the dark of the night, it was easy to follow. After she had walked a mile or so, she saw lights on an oil derrick that appeared to be far away. For the first time she realized that she had turned, not on a county road, but a temporary one built by an oil company. We are in the middle of a pasture! If I can't reach the lights, we may not be found before daylight. She turned toward the rig. The dark stillness broke from time to time by the soothing wails of coyotes. I am alone, she thought. All alone. Just me and the coyotes and jackrabbits hiding in the sagebrush. She thought about Joan walking around the house rehearsing her part in the senior play. *A lone. A looan. Awl Awl alooane.* Edward had teased, "If you tawk lik that you will be awl alooane."

She didn't feel despair or terror, but a supernatural calmness and a spiritual purpose as she struggled on. It never occurred to her that she hadn't walked a mile in quite a few years. Not since arthritis had slowed her step. She only panicked once. At the side of the road she saw a big black hole. She stopped. Is that hell? Is that a hole that leads to hell? Momentarily she was paralyzed by her thoughts. She crouched down in the middle of the road and inched forward to touch the frame of the ugly brute. After rubbing the edge, she realized it wasn't a hell-hole. It was a cattle guard. A black, freshly painted cattle guard. She had difficulty getting up, and it was painful putting weight on her knees, but she knew she had to go on. She looked ahead, sometimes hallucinating that she saw figures climbing on the derrick. It couldn't be. It was too far away.

Poor Muriel. Poor Joan. Poor Edward. *I've driven them up a wall. But you can't take my car keys. I'm perfectly capable of taking care of myself.* Emmaline was coming upon the fourth county mile marker when Muriel stumbled up to a highway. It was after two o'clock.

🖋 🖋 🖋 🖋 🖋

Edward had alerted the highway patrol. Within an hour there were three cars and a police helicopter searching for these independents, who always tried to keep a low profile.

Often they had taken a back road out of town so the weekly newspaper wouldn't publish in the *local* items, *Thursday, Muriel Watkins and Emmaline King visited the dentist in Ringgold.* This time they had taken a back road so they wouldn't have to backtrack.

🖋 🖋 🖋 🖋 🖋

The first car that approached Muriel simply passed her by. The next one came to a stop and the man rolled down his window.

"Please," Muriel said in a hoarse whisper, "our car is stuck and I need a ride to Littlefork."

"Lady, my kids are asleep in the back seat—but you stay right here and I'll stop at Littlefork and send someone out to get you." He rolled up the window and sped away. At Littlefork he saw the lights of the H and L Café and a patrol car parked outside. He went in and said to the patrolman, "There is a babbling, incoherent woman 'bout four miles up the highway, with blood on her face. Says her car is stuck. Looks pretty bad."

Four miles up the highway was where Benson Taylor, the patrolman, and an anxious Edward found her; scratched and battered, dried blood on her face and a lump on her forehead. The little corkscrew curls were frazzled, and the big brown eyes pleading. Her feet hurt so that she stood on the sides of them. She was, however, perfectly capable of telling them about where the car with Emmaline could be found. She pressed the quarter into Benson's hand. "You take this. I want you to have it."

"Your mamma's fine. I know she is," Muriel told Edward, as he lifted her up and set her on the back seat. "We'll find her."

A few minutes later they saw the car and found the note propped on the dash. Tayler radioed to the other vehicles in the search party to scour the area for Emmaline. Within five minutes or so they saw her, sitting by the side of the road. She was completely worn out. "I'm cold," she said, and they wrapped her in a blanket and carried her to the car. She squeezed her friend's hand as they were taken to the Greeenwood Hospital emergency room where they were given tetanus shots and had the burrs and stickers pulled from Muriel's feet.

"Next time," Emmaline whispered to Muriel, "we'd better stick to our guns. We'll count the miles."

"And watch for signs," Muriel said.

Joan and David had checked back at the H and L where the "posse" had set up headquarters. They learned the two women were safe, and would be spending the night at Edward's. They all finally got to bed about the time a brilliant sun burst over the hill. Emmaline's last thought before falling asleep was, *I hope nobody ever finds out about this. I hope it doesn't make the paper.*

The next afternoon Joan drove the ladies home in Emmaline's car, and Edward followed in hers. Over and over again, Emmaline said, "We could have made it just fine. We would have been found at daylight . . . but I know how much worry I caused you and Edward. I am sorry."

Of course, Joan was a little prissy and proper about it. "I told you not to drive, mother," she said at last.

"We made it, didn't we?" Emmaline replied.

"I give up," Joan snapped.

"And you'll leave us alone?" Emmaline asked quickly.

"Is that what you want?" Joan demanded, astonished.

"Oh, not to be left alone, exactly . . . but to be allowed freedom, dear . . . room. We're hardly children."

Joan grimly eyed the road ahead. It was going to take her awhile to fathom this, Emmaline thought. Yet with the right parenting, Joan might let her go yet.

"I'm just glad you're both okay," Joan said.

They lapsed into silence, and Emmaline sat studying her friend's face. "What are you thinking, Muriel?" she asked.

"Oh, I was just entertaining this victorious thought that is a little vexatious, too. Here we are, some might say, a little advanced in years—and we darn well have advanced, too. You know some people just seem to give up. We never will."

Emmaline mustered the facial equivalent of a sigh, knowing that Muriel had had another idea—and hoping next time round she would hear about it second hand.

🐑　🐑　🐑　🐑　🐑

They were lucky. The trip didn't make the *Red Oak Times*. Somehow, though, the word did get around. One afternoon shortly thereafter, Reverend McCord called on Emmaline. "Is there anything we can do for you? Help you in any way?" he queried.

"No, no." Emmaline said. "I'm fine. Just getting along fine . . . but I was thinking about calling you to see if you might look in on the Johnston youngsters. Their grandmother was a friend of mine. I hear they have troubles—maybe need a little help."

The Marriage Question

Joan K. Moore

*I*t started with a lie. We bound our friendship over a burger and guided each other through a maze of personal history. Margaret gave me more than I wanted. I gave her less.

I admired Margaret. I envied the smooth, successful appearance of her life: a good career, long, elegant legs, and hair that shone red in the sun. But she spent people as if she were heir to their souls.

She was married once to an airline pilot who invested in oil. She and the oil left him out there in the great blue, and now she goes from man to man. Sometimes the distance traveled to reach her is worthless. She doesn't get too close. She stands at arm's length with her hands out. And with little prompting, she will offer the woeful excuse, "because I am adopted."

I am small and dark and reticent with a need to be punished. I guess that's why I courted Margaret—and LeRoy, the last man before I vowed fidelity to John. I floated through my life on a sea of B & B and ladies'-night beer, going from man to man. Brother LeRoy, a sweet Georgia boy, said to me the last night we made love, "Oh, Cerene, you don't know what you mean to me." The next morning he married a girl with an address and a paycheck.

I knew what I had meant to them all. While LeRoy was saying his vows to the bourgeois bitch, I curled up in his old blue shirt, stiff from the line, and nursed a fifth of B & B. I was crashed at the Dog House, communal dwelling of a local bluegrass four called Coyote. Watching the fire in the woodstove, I toasted the satisfied couple and picked at the way I thought I should be feeling about LeRoy. To heal the wound, I played in my head a scenario wherein they died—killed instantly as they exited the parking lot of The Orange Blossom Express.

After LeRoy, my motto had become *BURN OUT. DON'T FADE AWAY.* John scoffed and called that "self-indulgent drivel, better left to Neil Young." I stopped sleeping in the alley behind Sipango, put away my backpack and began to reconstruct the mess that was my life. Each step was a giant step. From hell, up is up.

🐎　🐎　🐎　🐎　🐎

Margaret sealed our union on the night we met with the marriage question. Her green eyes narrowed to calculating slits as she asked, "Are you married?"

I hesitated. Making marriage the symbol of my worth, my success, I lied.

"Yes."

"Oh, really? How long have you been married?"

Was this an initiation rite of women? I searched her green eyes for a clue, and quickly calculated eight years. She took the answer and stored it away as if she were hungry and the answer her dinner.

Through the course of our divided relationship, Margaret called often for advice she never took and always the marriage question.

I counseled, "No," the night she called and said, "Cerene, I intend to get pregnant, but I'm not going to tell the father."

"Listen to me, Margaret. The Desiderata isn't working for you," I argued, the morning after some no-name freak escorted her from the Arcadia motel with a pillowcase over her head and a knife to her throat.

And I answered the marriage question.

With each nagging ring of the phone, my body tensed for flight. I was never good with numbers and I was afraid each time she asked I'd give the wrong answer. Because I didn't hold the freedom of a marriage license, I began to feed her invented anniversaries.

April 10, 1979. The day I watched John's blue eyes as he read *Five Acres and Independence* and knew he was mine.

July 4, 1979. The bathtub beer party.

December 1, 1980. The day I moved in with John.

I gave them all to her on different occasions, but still she asked. I began to suspect that she was not quite all right.

She was obsessed with getting a confession from me. I held fast to my answers, and she kept repeating the question.

I guess this might have gone on forever, but you know nothing does.

One night the phone screamed "Margaret" in my ear.

"Do you want to hear a story?" she wanted to know.

"Sure," I lied, one eye on the television screen and the other on the clock.

"I heard today that you've been having an ongoing eight-year affair with your boss. The source is reliable."

Silence.

"Who is the bitch, Margaret? The stupid bitch. Have you ever seen my boss? It's ludicrous. Why would she say such a thing about me?"

"What makes you think it's a woman? I can't reveal my source, but I'm sure John will be interested. She says you're not married."

I had nothing more to say. She and the question had become ugly to me. I hung up.

I went to John and told him about the marriage question. He called me a sinner and asked me to marry him.

November 11, 1988. The day John and I were married.

I received one last call from Margaret. I longed to hear the marriage question. The answer was ready, on my lips.

She asked, "Do you want to hear a story?"

What was this question? I looked at the clock. I hung up.

Life, Love, Marriage, Dental Molds

Steffie Corcoran

olly's husband George has been coming in to our
dental office for regular cleanings and the
occasional composite filling for a few years
before we first lay eyes on her. A really nice man,
George always very sincerely says, "How are you today,
Mrs. Highfeldt?" when he passes my spot in the
reception area on his way to Archie's examining room.
When he passes my way again on his way out, he never
fails to say, "Nice seeing you again, Mrs. Highfeldt," or
sometimes, "Have a nice evening." George is about thirty,
not flashy, an engineer of some kind at the Conoco plant
here in Ponca City, I believe.

I can only assume that during those years, George
Phibbs must have mentioned his wife to my husband
during one of those safe, polite conversations that occur
over and over again between dentist and patient. I do
know that *I*, tucked away in the waiting area, heard
nothing first-hand about her.

I see "Knight-Phibbs" in the 12:30 slot of the
appointment book that first day she comes in, but the
hyphen throws me a bit, and I don't connect her to
George Phibbs. She blows in at 12:50 or so, and of course
a patient this late is bound to throw us hopelessly off
schedule for the rest of the afternoon—you can't play
catch up in dentistry.

Very flashy. A full six feet or so of her, machine-tanned,
conspicuous white-blond hair, lots of makeup, carefully
and artfully applied with a heavy hand. And a manner
about her, the kind of manner that demands attention
and makes you wonder why she's working so hard to

demand it. I'd like to say I recognized the danger immediately, instinctively, but I am ashamed to confess that I thought to myself, *Foolish sort of woman,* nothing more.

So she blows in, as I said, late, and with a dark, bronzy lipstick on. Completely inappropriate for the dentist's. Archie's rubber gloves will be stained brown with a gold undertone, and so will his smock and very likely his forearms after he's finished with her, I think. The woman immediately plops herself down in the chair closest to my reception area, digs for and retrieves a compact mirror, and, concentrating, begins a focused pulling at various strands of her pale hair, I suppose to make it conform properly to its heavily-sprayed, artistically unkempt-looking style. "Mrs. Knight-Phibbs, I suppose?" I ask.

She looks up at me, long fingers poised mid-pull. "Yes?"

"You had a 12:30 appointment, I think?"

"Yes," she says again, frowning, "at least I think it was 12:30."

"That's right. 12:30," I repeat.

Her eyes open quite wide. "Oh my, am I late?"

At this moment Archie comes around the corner and says, "Goodness, Polly, not even late enough to mention. I should thank you. You gave me a few extra minutes to enjoy my lunch." Archie is laying it on a little thick. He always breaks for lunch at 11:30 a.m. (barring emergencies, of course); he had finished his leisurely lunch of a bologna sandwich and apple at precisely 11:47.

"Archie," I say, "you do have that double root canal at 1:30."

"Yes, yes, Myra, I know. Polly and I are just going to take some molds and have a brief consultation, and I'm sure Mr. Whitehead won't mind waiting a few minutes for his root canals." He pauses dramatically. "After all, nobody is in a *hurry* for root canals, are they?" He chuckles and beams at Polly. She chuckles and beams right back at him. I notice for the first time something a little different about her smile, a little off.

Archie has quite a way with his patients. It is well-known throughout Kay County that Archie is the finest dentist in Ponca City. "Come right this way, Polly," my husband beckons, placing his hand lightly on Polly's right shoulder as he directs her to Examining Room 1. Archie turns back toward me. "By the way, Myra, Polly is George Phibbs's wife."

This is news to me, especially since she doesn't at all look his type. I would have figured George for a nice girl-next-door type, genuinely blond and unobtrusively pretty, always punctual. But they say opposites attract, don't they?

Archie and Heidi, his dental assistant, work on Polly and work on Polly some more. From my desk, I can hear the conversations from the examining room, and the last 20 minutes or so of Polly's appointment sound like small-talk to me. And with Mr. Whitehead waiting!

Among other things, Archie compliments Polly's beauty, hair, bone structure ("Classic!" he exclaims. "If we can get these teeth corrected, you'll be perfect!"), and legs ("Have you ever modeled, Polly?" he actually asks.).

I enter the office to consult with Archie about some insurance paperwork, and he turns to me and asks "Myra, doesn't Polly have lovely legs? Why, she could be a model, couldn't she? So tall, so pretty."

I glance at Polly's legs, which are stretched out in front of her as she lies prone in the dentist's chair, a top mold setting in her mouth, Archie's thumbs applying firm pressure from underneath. Since Polly's khaki miniskirt leaves a good portion of her tan legs, unencumbered by hosiery, exposed, I say, "Yes, you do have lovely legs, Polly. Such long ones, too." I pause. "Archie has had a thing for legs ever since he fell hard for Betty Grable when he was a boy."

Archie gives me a dark look.

"Who's Betty Grable?" Heidi asks.

"A famous dancer and pin-up girl from World War II," I explain happily.

"Hyuh, hyuh, hyuh, hyuh," Polly laughs politely through her molds.

"You really do have pretty legs, Mrs. Knight-Phibbs," Heidi says enviously. Like me, Heidi is built sturdily, like a compact pickup truck.

I can feel Polly's eyes appraising my own legs. She doesn't look worried about the competition.

"I will admit," my husband says, "to being a connoisseur of legs, so I suppose that must make me an expert and my opinion about your legs, Polly, an expert opinion." He beams at Polly again, and she looks pleased with the compliment—as pleased as a woman can look with a dental mold in her mouth. I roll my eyes and leave the room.

At 1:48 Polly Knight-Phibbs emerges from Exam Room 1, again beaming, Archie's hand on the small of her back lightly pushing her ahead of him. "Well, Polly," he says brightly, "I'll see you again just as soon as I've had a chance to consult with Dr. Masters about your molds and your orthodontia."

"Oh yes, Dr. Highfeldt. I'm just so excited!" Again I notice something a little funny about her smile.

"I enjoyed our conversation very much, Polly. We must talk about writing again sometime." Archie seems very sincere.

"Oh yes," she says breathlessly. She has a very breathy voice. "And we'll have to talk about dentistry again soon, too!"

"Certainly, my dear, we will. I have a feeling you'll soon be one of my favorite patients!" Archie squeezes Polly's hand.

"How fun!" she manages to squeak before fluffing out the door.

Meanwhile Mr. Whitehead and I have been observing this exchange, eyebrows raised. It is now 1:52, a full 22 minutes after Mr. Whitehead's appointment was scheduled to begin. "I think Dr. Highfeldt is ready to see you now, Mr. Whitehead," I prompt.

"Ah, yes, Mr. Whitehead," my husband answers, "right this way, please."

🖋 🖋 🖋 🖋 🖋

"She doesn't look at all his type," I say as we get in the car to leave for the day.

Archie clips on his shoulder strap/seatbelt combination. "Who's that?" he asks.

"Polly Knight-Phibbs."

"Doesn't look George's type? No, I suppose you're right. She's a poet, you know. They never look anybody's type, except other poets'."

I'm wondering when Archie became an authority on The Way Poets Are. "No," I say, "I didn't know. What kind of poet is she?"

Archie huffs and looks a bit put out. "What do you mean? What kinds are there?"

"Obviously I mean is she a serious poet? Does she publish her poetry? Does she make a living at it? You know."

"Yes, she's a serious poet. She's working on her Ph.D. at UCAT."

"Well, that's interesting," I say, wondering why Archie is defending her and suspecting she's not far along in her Ph.D. "What's wrong with her teeth?"

"Oh," my husband says, "that's very complicated." He explains that Polly Knight-Phibbs accidentally knocked out her right upper lateral incisor when she was 12.

Apparently the dentist she went to at that time ("An imbecile!" according to Archie) suggested she do nothing and let her teeth gradually fill in the gap left by the missing incisor. Polly, like many young girls, was quite insecure about her appearance. She was horrified by the idea, but since money was scarce, her parents agreed with the dentist to let time take care of the missing tooth. As a result, all the teeth on Polly's upper right side gradually shifted leftward to accommodate the missing incisor. I realize this must be the reason her smile looks odd, off-whack: it leans, or at least her upper right teeth do, slightly inward. In addition, her teeth don't mirror one another properly. Her two front teeth, side-by-side, are fine, but to the opposite of her left lateral incisor, is, surprise! a canine.

Archie further explains that her lower teeth are textbook perfect. To top the whole thing off, Polly has recently been experiencing severe headaches, caused, in Archie's opinion, by the general leftward shift of her entire upper mouth's bone structure.

"What can you do for her?"

"Polly has a few options. Easiest would be to have an oral surgeon move the jawbone back a bit so the shift would at least stop giving her headaches. But that will only be a temporary solution; the teeth could very well continue to shift left and begin grinding on the bone again. And that lovely young girl can't afford to walk around with all her uppers leaning even more! It's already a considerable aesthetic problem for her."

"What would be best?"

"Well, we could go ahead with the oral surgery on the jawbone, then have Masters put her in braces to line all the teeth back up. In the meantime, the space where she lost the incisor will gradually reappear. Of course I'll have to extract the misplaced canine before the braces go on. As soon as the teeth are all back where they're supposed to be, I'll build a bridge with a new incisor and canine on it. That should take care of everything nicely."

"Sounds expensive."

"Oh, it will be, it will be. But Polly says she's ready for it. George's insurance will pay 80% if we claim it's medically necessary."

"Is it?" I ask.

Archie is clearly shocked. "My god, Myra, the poor woman can't be expected to walk around with a canine in her incisor's spot and no incisor at all for the rest of her life. For god's sake, there's a bicuspid in there now! It's an outrage!"

I think her smile just looks a little out of kilter, but to a dentist with integrity, situations like this one are an insult to the profession and should be remedied no matter the pain and cost—just as long as the patient can afford it. Archie uses a different line on his more financially challenged patients and those without insurance: "But who would want to tamper with that charming smile? My goodness, it's what gives your whole face *character*!" Regardless, the patient either leaves the office full of hope for his or her future smile or happy to be such a unique, charming individual, someone whose face has such character that even the *dentist* won't hear of altering it. Either way, Archie gets lots of referrals and loyal customers. As I've said, he has a way with his patients.

🐟　🐟　🐟　🐟　🐟

Archie asks me to call Polly Knight-Phibbs for a consult appointment two days later. By now her plaster dental molds are ready. When I first call her to set up the appointment, she tells me she will not be able to make it in for at least three days. She is, she explains, trying to finish revising her newest rondel, which is entitled "Lubricating without Waiting." "It's just not *quite* right yet," she confesses. No fool, I deliberately do not ask her what it is about. We set her next appointment for Thursday at 3:00.

🐟 🐟 🐟 🐟 🐟

My husband brings that woman's dental molds to bed for the first time that same night. "What are you doing, Archie?" I ask, startled. He has never brought molds into our *bed* before. Archie is a believer that all the mysteries of the dental universe are to be hidden within the various substances—mainly clay, rubber, and plaster—of dental molds. He occasionally scrutinizes them over 100% Bran or while watching PBS programming, but never in bed. At least not until now.

"Fascinating, aren't they, Myra?" he asks, pointing out just how obvious the leaning is when Polly's teeth are taken out of the context of her attractive though flashy face.

"It's a good thing she's a nice-looking woman, or those teeth would really stand out," I say. They *are* strange looking molds.

"The crowding is so severe here," he points, tapping the back teeth on the upper left side, "that she really must be having serious headache pain."

I kiss Archie on the temple. "Pain is pain. Don't let it bother you. It's your business to relieve pain, sometimes even to cause it."

"But this pain Polly's going through now is completely unnecessary! She should have had this taken care of when she was a young girl. It's just so sad."

I sigh. "She probably got used to her teeth, Archie. Most people do."

"My god, Myra, the poor woman has a canine where her incisor should be and a premolar where her canine should be! Think of it! She's a poet, Myra, sensitive to beauty. At least she's still young. I'm just so glad George had the good sense to bring her to me before this became an even more serious problem for her self-esteem."

I flip off Jay Leno in the middle of a Newt Gingrich skit and roll away.

"She's written poems about her teeth, Myra. Think of that. I'm so glad I'll be able to help her."

I doubt that "Lubricating without Waiting" is a dentally inspired piece and wonder archly if she has one entitled "The Leaning Tower of My Mouth" anywhere in her collection. While I try to fall asleep, I hear Archie tapping various spots on the molds. I finally drift off to the grainy sounds of fingers on plaster and of plaster teeth being forced gently and repeatedly to bite down.

🖋   🖋   🖋   🖋   🖋

She throws the door open with a flourish at 3:28 on Thursday afternoon. Archie, having absolutely run out of catch-up work to do, sits in the lobby reading the newest issue of *People*.

"I think I'm just a little bit early!" Polly exhales as she wriggles out of her denim jacket and pulls at her hair. I look back at her, left eyebrow raised. "I'm not early?" she asks. I lower my eyebrow, shake my head. "Oh, my, I thought my appointment was for 3:30!"

"Three o'clock, I believe," I reply, "but I'll check my appointment book again to make sure." Already sure, I glance at it nonetheless. "Yes, Mrs. Knight-Phibbs, 3:00 it was."

"Now, Myra," Archie says, placing the magazine back carefully so that it fits precisely into the right spot of the fan-shaped arrangement, "we all make mistakes, don't we? We'll just have to explain this miscommunication to our other afternoon customers. I feel sure they'll understand." He squeezes Polly's shoulder to emphasize his point.

I know full well that it will be I who explains it to them, while Archie and Polly sit in Exam Room 1 laughing and chit-chatting about dental options and contemporary poetry.

"Oh thank you, Archibald," she says. "I'm just such a scatterbrain."

Archibald? He doesn't bother to correct her. I roll my eyes dramatically, but neither looks my way.

🖋 🖋 🖋 🖋 🖋

Heidi pokes her head around the corner of the reception area while Archie and Polly are still consulting. "Mrs. Knight-Phibbs says she's written a poem about him!" Heidi gestures with her head toward Exam Room 1.

"About whom?" I ask, determined to at least appear uninterested.

"About Dr. Highfeldt!" she hisses, "about your husband. It's called 'Ode on a Dentist: Apostle of Symmetry.' She read it to us. It's *beautiful*," Heidi emphasizes, big-eyed.

I roll my eyes again. Archie doesn't need this foolishness. Or me.

🖋 🖋 🖋 🖋 🖋

"This dental problem has scarred her deeply, Myra," my husband says to me over pork chops, rice florentine, and new potatoes. "She feels so alone."

"But a poem about you, Archie? Really. Or perhaps you'd prefer that I call you Archibald?"

"Don't be catty, Myra. Have a little compassion. Your teeth are flawless; you didn't even need braces as a child. Polly is a grown woman!"

"Excuse me for pointing this out, my dear, but you're not exactly the stuff heroes of poetry are made of." Archie is one of those rapidly approaching 50 in a state of panic so abject that they try to camouflage their bald spots by parting their hair slightly above their ears and folding the remainder over the tops of their heads. He would be horrified to discover that anyone was on to this little trick. The spare tire and pronounced jowls only emphasize that age is, alas, catching up with him.

"Some see the inside, Myra. True inspiration is soul to soul, Myra." I can see by the sulky expression that I've hurt his feelings.

"Now Archie, I love the way you look, and I love you. But it is a little unbelievable that a beautiful young woman married to a wonderful fellow like George could be so inspired by her dentist."

"If it's all so ridiculous, why do you think she's become so attached to me?"

I sigh. "Nearly all your patients are attached to you, Archie. This one just happens to be the only melodramatic second-rate poet among them. Obviously her physical charms aren't lost on you, either. Don't think I haven't noticed." Archie gasps as if stabbed. "Which is precisely my point. This will end up just another patient-dentist crush, one that will fade away as soon as the bridge goes in and you're not useful to her anymore."

"Humph!" Archie snorts. "Shows what you know, Myra. Polly tells me our auras are more similar than any she's ever seen."

"You have your fun, honey," I say, rolling over. "I just hope this little crush doesn't cause you to get your feelings hurt." Really, *auras*?

Weeks pass. Polly's oral surgery and extractions come and go, and after her sutures heal, Fred Masters puts her in braces. Our own office procedures continue as usual. Since there will be no additional work for Archie to do on Polly's teeth until her braces come off, we maintain a more or less blissfully on-time record with our appointments.

This doesn't stop Polly, though. Fred Masters office adjoins ours (referrals are everything in this business), and every several weeks when Polly has her braces tightened she stops in to show Archie her progress. Giddy, he interrupts whatever he's doing (filling teeth, draining abscesses, extracting wisdom teeth) with whomever he's doing it to and takes her back to our business office. I look the other way, stay busy with reminder calls and paperwork, and affect an air of great unconcern. On her way out, she always graces me with a nervous, lavender smile (she's chosen plastic braces with a purple hue), and it's clear to my practiced eye that her teeth lean a little less each time I see her, and the space which is making room for the bridge widens almost imperceptibly.

Meanwhile, for reasons unclear to me, Archie continues to bring Polly's molds to beds from time to time. He has by this time memorized every feature of every tooth, every angle of irregularity. He now seems to be studying them only out of habit. Running his fingers lightly over the plaster surfaces has become, he tells me, a form of relaxation. He fondles the molds without even looking at them now, gazing off in the distance, his thoughts far away.

"You may never see more unusual molds again, Archie," I say one night.

He comes back from wherever he was. "What's that, Myra? Oh, no, I suppose not. No, Polly's new molds will look very much like anyone else's after the braces come off and the bridge goes in." He sighs heavily.

I can't resist asking. "And when will that be, Archie?"

"Six more months. Not long now." Another heavy sigh.

🐿 🐿 🐿 🐿 🐿

I discover that they actually *are* sleeping together when I find the poem folded neatly in Archie's smock pocket as I separate whites from colors one evening. He must have subconsciously intended for me to find it, this awful thing scripted by she of the leaning teeth.

The poem is entitled "Mission Impossible: Otherwise Known as Futile Fornication." It's been typed on a computer, and it has a handwritten inscription which reads "For Archibald Highfeldt, D.D.S." Several garish and childishly drawn hearts of various sizes surround the type. Guiltless, I smooth out the fold marks and read:

Other people's dentist husbands are the best
obsessions
possible. They get inside you, for a very
very short time, then
absolutely retreat,
taking a little of you with them,
just enough you know it's gone,
but never leaving anything—
except being inside you—
in their wake.

Other people's dentist husbands make the best
lovers imaginable. They make you scream
out loud for a very
very short time, then leave you
screaming inside from the memory
of really screaming.
Who else makes you scream?
Makes you come in a federal disaster area flood
of forbidden guilt
that feels like being reborn
into the death that comes when they go?

Her dentist husband's interest in me makes me want
to die. Hope he slips away into me again.
Soon.

✒   ✒   ✒   ✒   ✒

I admit, I was a bit taken aback at these bad erotic images of my balding, heavyset husband playing love-god to a flashy bottle blond pseudo-poet. I have been his wife for 27 years, after all. He has always suited me just fine, more than just fine, in fact, in the bedroom. Still, it is difficult to imagine him having such a torrid effect on a very silly woman in her mid-twenties. And why am *I* such a big part of this pornography?

I refuse to panic. Refuse. Refuse even to respond in any way to this piece of trash calling itself poetry. Yes, I admit to myself, my husband is having a torrid affair with an attractive though flashy woman young enough to be his daughter. A very long-legged woman young enough to be his daughter. A long-legged young woman who apparently finds pleasures of the flesh (sagging though it may be) quite appealing.

I know my husband, Archibald Highfeldt, D.D.S., and I know the course this foolishness will take. I plan to buy an exercise bicycle. I may even stop flossing, this very night.

Archie studies me carefully for hours after the laundry has come out of the dryer, is sorted and folded. I replace "Mission Impossible," folded precisely as it was before, in his now clean smock pocket. He must know I've seen it, but he says nothing, probably waiting for my reaction. But I say nothing. I do not have any type of fit or hysterical reaction or even pack any suitcases, his or mine.

✒   ✒   ✒   ✒   ✒

Archie must have told Polly it's likely I've seen the poem, because her behavior is semi-hysterical, with a great deal of frantic hair-pulling, the next time she stops into the office. She desperately tries to avoid me, but as I catch a glimpse of her tugging hard enough to detach hair from scalp and drifting rapidly toward Exam Room 1, I call out, "Yoo-hoo, Polly! In too big a hurry to say hello?"

"No, no, Myra, not at all." She twists a long, light-colored strand around a finger, then inserts the strand into her mouth, sucking on it gently.

"Come over here and show me your teeth," I say, beaming.

She dutifully plods over and opens wide.

"Those little beauties are really shaping up, aren't they?" She nods.

"How is George?"

"He's fine, Myra."

"Been writing any poetry lately?" I ask, innocent as can be.

"A little." She swallows hard. "I'm in a really, really big hurry, Myra. Can I just breeze back and speak with Archie for a sec?"

"Breeze on, my dear, breeze on," I say, the smile never leaving my face.

At home I pedal my AirDyne thirty minutes a night while Archie is gone, presumably thrusting violently upon Polly or vice-versa. I also, against my better judgment, avoid using the cinnamon dental floss in our medicine cabinet. While I pedal furiously, I visualize long, sleek, muscular and tanned calves wrapped around my husband's neck; occasionally a pedicured toe with a bronze-colored nail accidentally ruffles his folded-over hair, and his bald spot announces itself. Neither party in my fantasy stops, even for a moment.

The affair stretches on. In the meantime, George has come in for two cleanings. I assume he is in the dark, because he looks more or less happy and continues to greet me sincerely with his how are yous and have a nice evenings. During his last appointment, I overhear him telling Archie how much of an impression he has made on Polly. "She thinks you're the greatest thing ever. We're both really grateful to you for helping her. She's got so much more self-esteem now!"

"Er, well, uh, yes, certainly, George." Archie clears his throat and sounds just miserable.

I ride on each night, as do Archie and Polly in my visions.

🖋 🖋 🖋 🖋 🖋

The day rapidly approaches. Polly is finally to have her braces removed and her bridge put in. On the rare occasions when he is home, Archie is not himself. He carries Polly's molds with him wherever he goes, even into the bathroom. I suspect they're spending quite a bit of time together thinking over the significance of the upcoming big day and making big love, Polly's unbelievable legs wrapped easily around Archie's neck. She has probably written a whole series of poems about him by now, but I am grateful I haven't stumbled across any of them. I, miserable, think up likely titles for them while pumping away furiously on my bike, titles like "My Dentist Gave Me a Big Shot—of Love," "Sucking Can Build a Bridge," and "On Contemplating Archibald's Drill."

🖋 🖋 🖋 🖋 🖋

The big day arrives. Polly emerges from Exam Room 1 victorious, smiling broadly, confidently for her adoring audience. "*You're* the artist, Archibald, the true artist," she breathes, too overjoyed to be as careful as she should, "in every sense of the word." They share a meaningful, though dirty, little look.

And her teeth *are* perfect. Archie had done wonderful work on Polly. No one would ever guess that these big, sparkling white, absolutely straight teeth have ever been flawed in any way. Heidi rushes Polly's new molds back to Archie's office to set.

🖋 🖋 🖋 🖋 🖋

Archie drops me off at the house at 5:30, then leaves me, presumably due to a pressing carnal celebration with the toothy poetess. The time has come for action.

I go to the garage and remove Archie's smallest hammer from his toolbox. I've already bought a box of peanut brittle. A prop, but necessary. I enter the master bath, hammer in hand, and rest my left palm on the edge of the counter for support. Opening my mouth wide, I whack the hammer hard into my right lateral incisor and canine. It hurts, a lot. Reloading, I whack myself in the same two teeth again, and a terrific, blinding pain travels up the nerves of my mouth and settles just below my right eye. Probably by this time I've managed to cause enough injury that a root canal, at the very least, will be necessary. On strike number three, I connect. A diagonal-shaped chunk of my right canine flies off into the sink. Now I wait.

🖋 🖋 🖋 🖋 🖋

Archie comes in at 10:30, just as Jay is starting his monologue. He bursts into our bedroom clutching two small boxes—Polly's before and after dental molds—in his hand. "Good evening, Myra," he says.

"I broke a tooth on some peanut brittle," I say through my swollen mouth. "I waited for you to come home."

He runs to me, tossing Polly's boxes of dental molds on the bed. "What? Let me see. Open, please."

I open wide. Archie pokes at the broken tooth and asks me, knowing the answer, if I'm in pain. I say I am. My mouth throbs dully. "Well, darling," he says, "we'll have to give you some pain medication and get you in a temporary first thing in the morning. We can't do a root canal, you know, until we've gotten rid of any infection."

"I know," I say, holding my face.

Archie mixes me a hot salt water to gargle with, then

instructs me to take a codeine-laced painkiller. He joins me in bed, covering my cheek with his skilled, steady hand. Later, those same hands find other places in need of attention. We make love for the first time in weeks.

Afterwards, he says, his head in my lap, "Oh, darling, I've been such a fool!"

"Yes, Archie, you have."

"Can you possibly forgive me, Myra?"

"I think so." I feel cold air whistle through the sharp edge of my broken tooth as I speak.

🖎 🖎 🖎 🖎 🖎

The next night—after I've had my broken tooth x-rayed and crowned with a temporary—I lie down in our bed, still nursing quite a bit of pain, though the soft haze of codeine has blurred it some.

Archie kneels down by the side of the bed and takes my hand. "I have a surprise for you, darling," he says. He opens a small box labeled *Myra's Molds,* reaches inside, then pulls out a red squiggly something. Spread out in the palm of his hand, the rubbery pre-molding solution spells out a crimson *Myra* in Archie's crabbed physician's script.

"Oh," I say, as Archie puts his hand on my flannel-covered thigh.

"My goodness, darling, but you're firming up," my husband says to me.

Violin Music in the Night

Linda Marshall Sigle

*I*was normal until about the age of four. That's not very long to discover what normal is, so I could be wrong, but when I see this quartet of joggers daily in Couch Park, excuse my expression but I always think of them as the thundering herd of bitches, and each one has her hair bleached to the exact shade of blond as the others, same haircut in fact, now that I think of it, a sort of pageboy, and they talk incessantly of remodeling their houses. I look at them and think these are normal people. I'm not saying that when I was three-and-a-half I jogged and bleached my hair, but had not a momentous event happened at four, I might have been part of a thundering herd.

I discovered that somebody in the heat of a north Texas night, behind the forest green chain-link fence, past the graveyard of unclaimed bodies, played the violin, mournfully and slow, to pass the long hours of a darkness that would never end for him.

It was a time before Prozac, before Lithium, before Nortryptaline. A person came to the Wichita Falls State Mental Hospital and never left.

We came when I was four. My father took a job as the mechanical engineer. He brought us in the rain to see the white-frame house that was part of the benefit package. Rain is rare in north Texas. The dust of that day was buried under green for awhile. I was delighted to see cottontails in the backyard and jackrabbits beyond on the prairie. On two sides of the house was nothing but prairie, sloping away to a creek, rolling away from there to a cattle ranch, and finally running up against, miles away, a stock car race track. On summer evenings, we heard cows lowing, and in the distance, the engines as the cars circled around and around the track until midnight when the night was capped with a demolition derby.

In front of the house was another field, this one kept clipped by a tractor mower. We counted twenty-two jackrabbits on that stubby grass one evening. My older sister and I might have counted more, but one began to creep toward us, awkward and crab-like, and my mother, ever fearing rabies, brought us inside.

On the kitchen side was my collie's yard. His fence of livestock paneling was so burdened with trumpet vines that it ceased to be airy and became more of a green rampart. Beyond that was a graveyard behind barbed wire. The stones had numbers instead of names. Beside the cemetery was a tennis court. Past the tennis court were rows of wards, where patients stayed in great hallways of rooms where metal beds were lined up in rows as neat as those in the graveyard. When the inhabitants couldn't bear that sight anymore, they went to the long balconies that were fenced in by green painted chain-link. There they walked around and around like cats in a zoo.

But on that rainy day in 1959, it seemed like a preschooler's paradise.

This Eden lasted for quite a few years. Raccoons came in through the cat's door. They would reach their hands toward us to take kibble from our stubby, youthful hands. My father built a wooden sandbox where I imprisoned box turtles. I loved them so. In the evenings I brought them lettuce and canned dog food. I made for them a miniature lake to drink from. I did everything that I thought might amuse the twenty or so turtles I had. But when they weren't sleeping under the seats, they were walking the inside perimeter of the box, always looking up, thinking an escape route would eventually appear. The wood finally rotted. They made their slow dash to freedom.

At five o'clock p.m., the non-violent patients, who were free to roam in the daytime, were locked up. At that minute, my mother set Sandy, my sister, and me free. We rode our bicycles around in circles on the tennis court. Sometimes we would be brave, escape the tennis court and ride through the streets between the wards. As we passed, hands would wedge out between the chain links, trying to touch our youthful freedom. Tinny voices called for us to come and take their hands. We pedaled away, fast. We pedaled to the entrance. Oddly enough, we never pedaled out the gate and to the neighborhood just across the street. We didn't live there.

Something happens about the time the pituitary gland blossoms. It pumps estrogen and testosterone into adolescent bodies, sure, but I think some kind of mean hormone starts flowing, too. For years nobody at school mentioned my home. Sixth grade came. It's a hard year, anyway. It's the year that you figure out that the underarms you smell may be your own, the time when you know you need a bra but can't figure out for the world how to measure yourself for one. It's a bad year to discover that you are different.

All it took was a cute boy, whose crewcut came to a swirl on the back of his head, to ask me where I lived. A girl, who was already lightening her hair with Summer Blonde, glared at me. With a sneer she said, "She lives at the mental hospital."

Suddenly I realized that when people called me, an operator, not me, answered saying, "Wichita Falls State Mental Hospital. What extension, please?" When I filled out the forms at school, I was the only one writing on the address line, "Wichita Falls State Mental Hospital, Box 300." One true sentence, said with a curled lip, made me realize I could bleach my hair, too, I could wear the fashionable white lipstick, I could know every word to every Beatles song, but I would never be normal in that cusp called Junior High.

And I would no longer sleep at night.

Somebody else could not sleep. As I lay awake in my strange bed that was built into the wall, the slow strains of a violin floated into my room. Being in the wall, I couldn't stare at the ceiling. I just laid there with sheet rock about two feet over my head. My sheet rock surrounded three sides of me. Into this stillness drifted that wail of longing. Night after night he played. Sometimes I awoke to hear my sister, also in the wall but above me, sobbing along to the music. The violin song didn't make me sad, but comforted me. Somewhere there was somebody who had something to do besides walk in circles, looking for an escape. The escape was in his hands.

My escape was in my hands, but my instrument was a pen.

Right before I turned thirteen, my father took a job at a paper mill in the south. The humidity was like a wall. The trees were thick and tall, so we couldn't see miles away where cows walked in single file or cars chased each other around an oval.

I was free at last. I wore double knit miniskirts like the other girls. My hair was the same shade of blond as theirs. Though I hated loafers, I bought them because they had them. But they seemed to know.

Those women in the park, the herd, I suspect, but I don't know because I'm not sure what normal is, but I picture them at night going to Junior League, to Tiara glassware parties, maybe taking a class on choosing colors for their remodeled homes. Maybe, but I don't know.

For some reason, I take night classes on deviant behavior. I take classes on the mental state of people locked up. When I'm not in class, I play a tape of violin music, and I write through the night.

" . . . Bitter Chocolate
Bitter Chocolate
Blood like ice water
Kisses taste like snuff
Why are all of my women
so jive and full of stuff . . . "

—*Ishmael Reed*

Produce

Benjamin Bates

*I*n my dreams I have a crazy brother. He howls at the moon. He lives with my mother on a quiet street. He prowls around in front of the house on hot humid summer nights, wearing a wool sweater and a too-small (three inches of the thick, black sweater sticking out from its too-short sleeves) leather jacket, zipped to the neck. He waves his arms and points his finger.

I come by to visit one night. My crazy brother is on the lookout. He is getting fat. His pants stretch across his hips, stop above his ankles. He wears lime green socks. I can see my mother pacing back and forth in the front window. Are those tears? Her face is contorted. I put my arm around my brother and ask him to come inside. He pushes away from me. He takes a ball peen hammer from under his sweater and comes at me.

🖎   🖎   🖎   🖎   🖎

"You are in mortal danger." I thought it was a joke. That one sentence, on the back of one of those pink phone message sheets, in my mail file by mistake. I work Produce at National Grocery, corner of Herkimer and Cherry. The place is vast—a superstore. We have a bunch of strange cases working at National. I didn't think the note was for me. It didn't have my name on it. I threw the note away.

"You are in mortal danger." I had just been promoted to assistant produce manager, so when I got the second note, a couple weeks later, that one sentence written on the back of an employee newsletter, I figured it was somebody who didn't like affirmative action. I started snooping around the store for suspects. I still thought it was a joke, but it wasn't funny. I showed it to my wife that night.

She said, "I sent it."

"Stop lying. You haven't been to the store."

"Mailed it."

"That's not your handwriting."

"I had my hitman sign it."

"This is serious!" I told her my suspicions.

She laughed. "The slack-jawed yokels who work at National couldn't even spell 'affirmative action.'"

"What has that got to do with the note?"

"You don't have to raise your voice, Arnold."

"What has . . . ! Slack-jawed yokels?!"

"Lisa Simpson said that to somebody."

"Who is Lisa Simpson?"

"Arnold, please. Lisa Simpson on *The Simpsons*. You need to get in touch. The whole world is not produce."

I *am* obsessed with produce. I love pears. When my daughter was three, she hated pears. I would get up with her every morning, slice a pear and make her eat half. She was a tough little bird. She hated pears, but she would eat them anyway, all the while telling me how much she hated pears. "They're good for you," I'd say. "You're going to love pears." This went on for weeks. Then I brought some bananas home, and told her she couldn't have any. She begged and pleaded. Cried herself to sleep that night because I wouldn't give her a banana. The next morning I woke up and found her curled on the floor, watching a cartoon, eating a banana. When I called her to come and eat a pear with me, she took a big bite of her banana. My first born.

She's nine now, still too young to understand that her victory was really mine. Some mornings she still catches my eye, takes a bite of her banana—it might be a mango, or kiwi fruit; she likes that exotic stuff—and gives me a little sneer. I love pears.

🐎   🐎   🐎   🐎   🐎

I found my Aunt Trudy hiding behind the La-Z-Boy with the left side of her face caved in. She's a high-toned woman but the left side of her face was flushed purple. Blood oozed at the corner of her mouth and her lips looked royal. Her left eye was closed. She sucked air through the right side of her mouth. Aunt Trudy is my Uncle Ed's wife. I don't know what she was doing in my dream, but there she was, behind the La-Z-Boy holding a butcher knife. You could tell she wasn't going to use it. Some people pick up a weapon because they have no inner strength, but even with guns in their hands these people look weak. Aunt Trudy had that kind of look on the right side of her face. She wasn't going to use that butcher knife. I was helping her up from behind the chair when Uncle Ed comes in from the kitchen. He says, "You want a sandwich?"

I say, "What the hell did you hit her with?"

"I slapped the taste out of her mouth," he says. He laughs.

🐎   🐎   🐎   🐎   🐎

Let me tell you about Carla Bone. First, I'm not fucking her. People find that hard to believe, but it's true. Carla is a living, breathing white man's fantasy: short, tightly curled hair that lies flat against her head when she straightens it, dark chocolate skin, thin brows, wide brown eyes, broad nose, full lips, full hips, and something in the way she moves makes it hard just to watch. But she has bad taste in men. She'd probably be better off fucking me, married and all, but it ain't happening.

My wife asked me about Carla once. She come into the store about two weeks after Carla came to Produce, which was maybe eighteen months ago. Shocked the hell out of me, because my wife *never* comes to Produce. Anyway, she come into Produce one day and then that night in bed she asked if I wanted to fuck the new produce handler.

"Now why would you ask me that?"

"Answer the question."

"You shouldn't ask the question if you don't want to hear the answer."

"I wouldn't."

She was stroking me when the conversation started, so I tried to roll on top of her, but she resisted. "Answer the question."

"You mean, like in a threesome?"

"Stop bullshitting."

"What? You don't want to fuck her? I thought everybody wanted to fuck Carla Bone."

"Everybody except you, right?"

"Yeah. That sounds good."

"You better get serious with me."

I had her down, but she wouldn't spread. "This is as serious as I get."

"Then I guess nothing is happening."

I rolled off. "Why do you do this?"

"What am I doing?"

"Do you want to make love or not?"

"That was the question I asked you."

"I come home to you every night."

"What has that got to do with anything?"

"It means I love you. It means I want to be with you. It means I'm not looking to be with anybody but you."

"Would you please just answer the question?"

I rolled away from her. With my back to her I said, "No."

Carla is my friend. Men can have female friends. I taught Carla how to slice a watermelon. We sell halves, quarters, even watermelon wedges and fruitboats, and Carla couldn't make clean cuts. At first I thought she was doing it on purpose, because when you make a bad cut you end up eating most of the heart yourself, but Carla don't even like watermelon. She just needed help with her technique. She has good hands. Handles grapes like a charm.

Carla ain't no schoolgirl but she's a sucker for sweet talk. I've seen it happen. This last dude come right into Produce and picked her up. Come into the store one day dripping with drug money: grey silk and wool double-breasted pinstripe over a black tank top, hair curled, gold hoop in his right ear, three gold ropes around his neck, diamond on the left pinkie to match the one in his left ear—couldn't be no more than seventeen, eighteen years old. I wanted to grab him by his ankles, turn him up, shake him and watch all the little white rocks spill out. Come into Produce all by himself. Had her weigh him up some grapes, then ate the whole bunch while he followed her around talking. Waited while she went in the back a couple times. Toward the end she was staring at him, smiling and pouting at the same time. When he left she kissed him.

Later I asked her, "So are you going to adopt him?"

"Do he look like he need a mother?"

These women all try to be so flip. Want to show how independent they are, but that's a dead end. Look at Oprah Winfrey. Don't get me wrong. I admire the woman. Oprah Winfrey made fat black women all over the world feel better about themselves. Oprah proved that you do not have to be thin and blonde and white to be smart and rich and famous. But here she is with all this money, still trying to lose weight. And that nigger she's always talking about, that she takes all her pictures with? Steadman? Whatever. Brother at the barbershop calls him "Instead-of-a-man." If that was really her nigger, she'd be big as a house and couldn't care less about her weight. And who she going to leave all that money to? She ain't got no kids. Oprah getting on up there, too. Her biological clock is about to explode. She'll be all right, she got enough money to hire her some kids if she want to. But I bet she'd rather do it the old-fashioned way. When you get down to it, that's what they all want. I mean, what else could Carla Bone want from this young boy?

"Hey, yo, Pops! You seen Carla?"

I'm finishing up my display of mustard greens when he walks up. Before I come to Produce, National didn't even carry greens, but now we got mustard, collard, turnip greens by the bunch, kale, too. I'm proud of my greens.

"Yo, Pops. Fruitman."

I've been called worse, but the way he said it was like he wanted to spit. I turn on him. He's all done up in the purple and orange of the Phoenix Suns: Charles Barkley ripping down a rim on his tee-shirt, geometric stars and letters on the jacket, which is purple with one orange sleeve, purple over-the-knee baggy shorts with an orange ball of fire at the crotch.

"What time is the game?"

"Say what?"

"Is Barkley playing tonight? I heard he was hurt."

"Man, please. You seen Carla?"

"She got off." I look him dead in the face now, to see if he gets my drift. It's a narrow, soft face, almond colored. His eyes remind me of my mother's. His shoulders are narrow, and his legs are too skinny for his huge black and purple Nikes. Maybe that's where he keeps his rocks. I was about his size when I was a kid, but I've filled out some since I got married. I could take this boy. "She been gone half an hour, forty minutes."

He stares through me. "She said meet her here at three."

Carla went in the back not five minutes ago, but I don't like this kid. "Y'all must have got your signals crossed. You was doing the pick-and-roll, she was doing the pick-and-pop."

Just then Carla comes out from the back looking like the freshest thing in Produce. "Hey, baby," she says, and gives him a kiss. "How you doing?"

"Just cooling with the Fruitman," he says. Doesn't even look my way as they leave.

First and last thing every shift, I rearrange the pears. We've got a sale on this week. Bosc, Bartlett, Northwest, Comice, Seckel, all 59 cents a pound. They're piled in the bins looking beautiful. I love the colors and the textures and the smells. I'm standing there inhaling and studying the blemishes when I notice that the little plastic pocket just above the bins, where we keep the recipes, is a mess. We have instructions for dishes like spiced pears (chopped Bartletts, mixed with sugar, cloves, ginger and cinnamon, all of it brought to a boil and simmered— delicious) on 3X5 cards that stay in the pockets for weeks because the customers never notice. But today the recipes have taken a beating. I pull out a few of the crumpled ones and find a plain white index card amongst them. It has one line typed on it: "You are in mortal danger."

That's when I knew it was Carla. I mean, whoever was leaving the notes had to know my habits. I figured that somehow she was using this young boy to get to me. It didn't make much sense, but women do crazy things when they want a man. I was flattered for a moment, but then I got angry. Did she really think I would leave my wife and kids for her? Did she think her stuff was that hot? Here I was trying to be a friend to the woman, but she figures all I want is to get in her draws. That's what all men want. These women can be so stupid. But then I blame Oprah for that, too.

🖎 🖎 🖎 🖎 🖎

I hear voices behind an almond-colored door. I'm a little boy, pressed against the door, trying to get to the voices, but I can't turn the knob. Someone—my sister?—is sobbing and breathing in loud gasps. I hear my mother, too: angry, rasping. Then a third voice, deep and sullen. I keep reaching for the knob, turning it, turning it. My penis, rubbing against the almond door, begins to swell. When I wake up I can never remember how old I am, but I guess little boys get hard, too. I sink to the floor, playing with myself, my back to the almond door, when suddenly it opens. The man who told me to call him Daddy kicks me in the back of the neck as he exits, and tumbles over me. "God Damn!" he snorts.

My mother is right behind. "Where the hell do you think you going?"

My screams drown out my sister's sobs. She comes to pick me up. She presses me against her wet, heaving chest.

"I said, where you going?"

The man who told me to call him Daddy brushes dust from the knees of his pants. "To the corner," he says. "I need a pack of cigarettes."

As he leaves my mother yells after him, "Bring me back a loaf of bread!"

＊　＊　＊　＊　＊

My six-year-old son cussed his teacher today. Told the bitch to go to hell. Naturally, the teacher is thinking, "What kind of parents—? What kind of home training—? Blah, blah, blah . . . ." I don't use foul language. You don't believe me, just like you don't believe I'm not fucking Carla, but that's on you. Foul language is everywhere. A kid ain't got to get it from his parents. Everybody from Martin Lawrence to David Letterman is saying ass and bitch and damn and hell. I do not use foul language. Not around my kids, anyway.

And as for home training, point one, my kids have a mother *and* a father. Couple years ago one of Fannie Lou's teachers was so surprised to see me at Open House, she pulled me to the side and asked if I could meet her for a drink. People see this single father nonsense on TV and believe it. I told her I'd check with my wife and get back to her. Just so happened my wife was in class herself that night. She's getting her master's from City U. The title of her thesis is "Homer Simpson: A Hero for the Common Man."

Which leads to point two: we want our children educated, so we make sure their homework is done, their hair is combed, their clothes are clean and their bellies are full every single morning. And I don't hesitate to show my face at school—class parties, assemblies, PTA, whatever. My wife the same way. Our kids ain't perfect, but they ain't bad.

"So you'll go up to school to talk to her?"

I have a ritual. Every night after work I go to the bedroom (this is after half an hour of wrestling on the floor and listening to rapid-fire reports of the day), sit at the foot of the bed, hit the urban contemporary channel on the cable music station, kick off my shoes and socks, and massage my feet. If the massage takes less than fifteen minutes, I'm moving too fast. My wife's voice comes to me just as I start to scratch my toes.

"Arnold? Will you talk to her?"

"Why me? I don't have time to be running up to that school."

"Why not? The fruit won't spoil."

"Why can't you go?"

"I have to see my thesis advisor tomorrow. If I don't have this degree by May, I'm subject to kill one of those bastards."

"Go Friday, then. Y'all could work it out woman-to-woman." My toes are tingling.

"Somebody should be up there tomorrow. We can't just let it sit. Besides, I hate that bitch. Me and her get together, it's a fight. I might have to snatch her weave."

"I'm going to tell Ms. Farmer how Marcus learned to cuss. And didn't you insist on putting him in her class?"

"Oh, she's a good teacher. She's a very good teacher. But she been working with little kids too long. I ain't no little kid."

"And what am I?"

She turns from her dresser and stands over me, her hands on my shoulders, pressing my nose between her breasts. "You're my man. You take care of things." She kisses between my eyebrows, rubs my head, squeezes my shoulder, then turns back to her dresser. She is on her way to class. My toes are screaming.

"If she's such a bitch, how do we know he was wrong? You know how Marcus is. Maybe she did something, and he had to tell her off."

"Marcus is a six-year-old boy."

"That don't mean nothing."

"It means he should do what the teacher tells him to do."

I hate how the brother is always in the wrong. People don't even want to know the circumstances. The brother is guilty, open and shut. Here's my boy in the first grade, already an outlaw. The brother lives his whole life wearing a bullseye. I used to feel that way about my father, until I realized he wasn't my father.

You have to understand how I grew up. We lived in the projects. Grown men were like, shadows. On our floor there were two. One was my friend Cookie's stepfather, but he was in and out of jail. Then there was Damion, who lived in the corner apartment with his mother, but when she died, he got strung out and started wearing her dresses. My biological dad died when I was about three. I never knew anything about him.

When I was five or six, Mr. Robinson moved in. He was going to be the man of the house. Wanted the kids to call him Daddy. I thought it was cool, but I was the baby. My sisters were both teenagers and my brother was already running wild. My sisters still talk about Mr. Robinson, how he was going to make everything "shipshape" except he didn't have a boat. Mostly I remember a lot of shouting. Between him and my sisters, and then later between him and my mother. One day he was just gone. I think I was eight.

My mother kept a shoebox full of snapshots. She could sit with my sisters or a couple of her friends and shuffle through old pictures for hours. Creased, cracked, faded, over-exposed, under-exposed, out-of-focus, off-center old pictures. When I was a teenager, if I saw my mother go for the shoebox I went the other way. Then she died three years ago, and I was sitting with my sisters after the funeral. I come across three or four shots of the same guy while we're flipping through the shoebox.

"Who's he?"

"You don't know who that is?" My sister Ludie would always rather confirm my ignorance than answer my questions. "You really don't know who that is? Do you hear this boy, Mary?"

My sister Mary is the oldest. She is approaching three hundred pounds. She speaks only when the conversation comes to her. "That's your Daddy."

"That don't look like Mr. Robinson."

"You damn right it don't." Ludie is suddenly hot. She dabs at the beads of sweat on her nose. "That's your real Daddy, fool."

I take another look. The man in the photo looks like John Lee Hooker, the blues man. He has a look of mischief in his eye. He holds a shot glass in his left hand, as if he is toasting the camera. Something dark—maybe his hat—is in his hand. One corner of his mouth is turned down. Must have been his way of smiling. "How come—?"

"That damn Robinson made Mommie take his pictures down. He said he wanted her to stop living in the past. Asshole. I'll never know what Mommie saw in him. He was too young for her. He called, you know. 'I heard about your mother . . .' Son of a bitch. I hung up on him."

"Ludie—"

"Don't even start, Mary. You hated him too."

"But how come nobody told me—?"

"What was there to tell?" Mary is the voice of wisdom. She has managed my mother's funeral with complete calm. "He was good while he lasted."

I'm not one for pictures. Nothing in my wallet, nothing in my locker at work. I don't need to be reminded how my kids look. I see them every day. But I kept that shot of my old man, to remind me that things don't last. That's why I'll have to get out of here early tomorrow and run some interference for my boy Marcus. Can't have Ms. Farmer getting down on him. I'll have to call Carla—

I spring off the couch. "You are in mortal danger."

When the room stops spinning I look at my watch. Almost midnight. The kids have taken their baths and gone to bed. My wife has returned from her class. All I remember is watching the start of *Law and Order*: three young brothers caught in a drug deal, a cop shoots one of them and puts a gun in his hand.

Before I know it I'm in the kids' room, standing in a heap of underwear and towels and clothes and books and papers and toys. Fannie Lou's arm hangs down from the top bunk. Marcus looks to be sleeping on his knees. I hold my breath trying to hear theirs.

My wife is sitting up in bed with a book. She looks up as I enter the room. She wants me tonight. The look in her eye makes me exhale, as if I had been ready to burst.

"Arnold? You look like you seen a ghost."

All I can do is laugh.

🐾　🐾　🐾　🐾　🐾

The worst one is when the babies are falling. I'm in a football game, like I just took a big hit, and I'm flat on my back looking at the sky through the bars of my helmet, just as it starts to rain. The raindrops come from far, far away; as they fall they darken and swell. I hear babies crying, and then I hear them crashing into the Astroturf all around me. I scramble to my feet, still dizzy from the hit, and stumble around trying to catch the babies.

🐾　🐾　🐾　🐾　🐾

I have to see Carla face-to-face. I'm going to be late for work, with nobody to cover for me, so I'm a little pissed off, which is not quite the right mood for Ms. Farmer, but I go by the school anyway. The woman must be six feet, with shoulders as broad as mine. Her face is cosmetic—burnt red eyeshadow and bright red lips. She warbles when she talks. You think she's going to finish every sentence with "Do you understand?" like when the cops bust somebody, but she never does. I'm thinking my wife could never jump high enough to slap her, but somebody should. Not me. I nod and promise that Marcus will clean up his act. And I remind her that Marcus is somebody's child.

I get to Produce and we've got what looks like a ton of almonds boxed up in back, and no place to put them on the display floor. Mr. Strajchan, the produce manager, has made a special deal. He wants to put the almonds in one-pound bags and line them up between the display stalls. Mr. Strajchan thinks the almonds will move like wildfire at 89 cents a pound. Of course, since I'm late, Carla hasn't shown up, and Strajchan, Jr. is above bagging, the produce manager's plan is running behind schedule. I'm at my locker getting into my apron when I feel the heat.

"You're going to spend the whole day bagging nuts, son."

"Looking forward to it, Mr. Strajchan." (The name is pronounced "strawn." I had worked Produce for three months before I learned to ignore all them letters in the middle.)

"Where's your assistant?"

"You mean your son?"

"I'm talking about Bone."

"Haven't heard from her."

"I thought you two were keeping company."

"Just co-workers, Mr. Strajchan."

"Give me a break, Garris. You mean to say you're not hammering that nail?"

"I don't understand what you mean."

"Never mind. Just get those nuts bagged."

"Yes, sir."

Carla never shows. I spend the rest of the morning swimming in almonds. About noon Strajchan reports that she called in sick. Just before quitting time she calls again.

"What's been happening?"

"Where you been? I been shifting nuts all over Produce but nobody's buying. And Strajchan is steamed."

"I can handle Strajchan with a wink."

"That don't work for me."

"Can you come by my place tonight? I have a surprise for you."

"What kind of surprise?"

"It's nothing bad. For real. It's good. But I want to tell you in person."

"Yeah. I got some news for you, too."

I didn't even check the pears on my way out. I got lost on the way to Carla's place, too busy planning my speech to watch the street signs. When I was younger I had trouble brushing a woman off, but I though this would be easy. Usually when you say you just want to be friends it's a lie, but this time I really meant it. I'd tell Carla that I wanted her friendship more than I wanted that great body. And that the notes just had to stop.

When I parked near Carla's building I saw her come out on the porch with the kid I had seen in Produce. They embraced, then she clutched his hand and kissed it. He came down the steps and passed on the sidewalk in front of me while I sat in my car. His thin frame was engulfed in a hip-hop ensemble: Levi's as baggy as David Brinkley's eyes, blue-green plaid shirt hanging nearly to his knees, a skullcap with the long tail, a bandage across his nose and black streaks under his eyes like the football players wear. The sight of him is still in my head as I enter Carla's apartment. She blindsides me before I can get in a word.

"I want you to go on the Oprah Winfrey Show with me."

"What?"

"She's doing a show on 'Men Who Work Well With Women.' I called in your name. You been so good to me, Arnold. On the job, I mean."

"What?"

"She did a show last week on sexual harassment. Some guy got up there and say a lot of guys treat women with respect, and Oprah ought to do a show about that, instead of always bad-mouthing the men."

"The Oprah Winfrey Show?"

"Then the next day they put an 800-number you could call if you had a good story about a man on your job. I called in your name."

"You—?" The Oprah Winfrey Show?"

"They're taping the show tonight! They're coming to take us to the studio in a limousine!"

"We're going to be on Oprah? For real?!"

She sprang into my arms and hugged me. I though she would kiss me, but she stopped, and a puzzled look came over her face. She pulled away from me. "You watch Oprah?"

"Damn, Carla. Everybody watches Oprah. You think my whole life is Produce?"

"I didn't think— I didn't think—" Her eyes were downcast.

"They're sending a limo? When?"

Suddenly she smiled. "They said it would be here in an hour."

This time I hugged her. "You got us on Oprah! Well, I'll—'Men Who Work Well With Women.' Damn right!"

Carla looked me dead in the eye, and I thought for sure she would kiss me, but she didn't. "You deserve it," she said.

"I need to call my wife!"

I've been with my wife since high school. Twenty years.

She picks me up when I'm down, and I do the same for her. We love each other and everything, but some things she just don't understand. She works so hard to keep me from getting the big head, she forgets that every now and then I might want a little recognition. I treat her with respect, she acts like she's entitled. I do a good deed, she suggest two or three more I could do when I get a chance. I slip just the slightest bit off the straight and narrow, the suspicion never stops. But Oprah is once in a lifetime.

"Did you forget Fannie Lou's recital?"

Ms. Ntozake Zulima's Ballet, Jazz, and Modern Dance Studio. Classes for every level, from Beginner to Professional. Recitals on the third Thursday of every month. How could I forget. "Is that tonight?"

"Every third Thursday."

"But this is Oprah!"

"Let me get this straight. You call me from your girlfriend's house, to tell me you're going to miss your daughter's recital, so you and your girlfriend can tape a television show."

"Yeah. That sums it up."

"Since when did Oprah start taping at night?"

"How should I know?"

"When will this show be on?"

"I don't know! They're sending a limo!"

"Somebody is trying to make a fool of you, Arnold."

"What?"

"That's what they do on talk shows. Ordinary people get in front of the camera and make fools of themselves."

"This is about 'Men Who Work Well With Women.'" Carla called in my name cause I helped her on the job. You're a working woman. Or at least, I hope to hell you will be, if you ever get out of school. You should want to see good role models on TV."

"And you're a good role model?"

"You married me. What do you think?"

"I think somebody is trying to make a fool of you."

≈ ≈ ≈ ≈ ≈

Sitting in a bald-bulb mirrored glare. I turn, and somebody dabs my face with a powderpuff, setting off a fine, dry, white spray before my eyes. A television image swims toward me from across the room. I float through a door. Unlike the dressing room, the studio feels cold, and smells like raw meat. I'm surrounded by Oprah's attendants as I drift toward the stage. They mike me up, anchor me to a chair, give me a last dab of powder. Then a producer hands me a note. I grab her hand and shout, "Where's Carla?" but she snatches her hand away and rushes backstage as a blast of Oprah's music fills the room. I crumple the note in my fist as camera lights flood the stage.

Oprah's voice is an electric current on the air. I see her as if I'm looking through flame. Oprah paces, the audience massed behind her. She stops, and Carla Bone, wearing a wild feverish expression, a black choir robe and a huge cross, appears next to her. Then Carla rushes the stage, heads straight at me, and at the last instant she cuts to her left, like Jerry Rice running a post. I fall out of my chair. Prone, I look across the stage and see Carla kneeling at the feet of the kid from Produce. His black robe is just like Carla's, only the sleeves and the collar are iridescent. His cross is even bigger.

I scream, "Who the hell are you?!"

"Say hello to your son!" Oprah shouts. "Those who saw it may remember a program we did about a month ago, that featured the charismatic evangelist who is known only as the Leader. This wonderful young man has a special ministry to preach against teen pregnancy. His special gift is to speak to the youth in their own language.

He is truly one of them—the "illegitimate," the abandoned, the bastard. I too confronted these terrible labels when I was a young person. His personal quest has been to find the man who abandoned his mother when she was a teenager. The deadbeat, er, the man on our stage!" The audience roars.

The kid smiles. "Do the name Ruby Begonia ring a bell with you?"

Ruby Begonia. Also known as the Big Easy. Also known as Rebecca Barrow, a girl in my homeroom, junior year. How could I forget. "My son is at home with his mother."

"He can't answer the question, Oprah. He can't face his responsibility."

"But—"

"You ignored my notes. Just as you've ignored me all these years! He knows the truth of my words, Oprah. I am God's channel on Earth!"

"Enriched with the power of syndication!" Oprah sings.

The kid stands between Oprah and Carla. They look as if they want to lift him to their shoulders.

I feel the crumpled note from Oprah's producer in my hand. I throw it across the stage and charge after it. "I'll show you who's in danger, you spoiled little—You son of a—"

Then Oprah's voice explodes: "Time for a break!" Have to go to a commercial. We'll be right back!"

Before I can reach them the studio goes black.

🖋 🖋 🖋 🖋 🖋

The day after the show I took off work and drove to the Finley Park Institute for the Criminally Insane. My brother's been there for five years, since he killed my cousin Emory. The two of them got drunk one night and got to arguing over some girl. I sit on a folding metal chair and listen. My brother tells of the days when he served with Che Guevara in the Colombian jungles. He reminds me that he also served with Black Jack Pershing when the General chased Pancho Villa through Mexico. On both campaigns, my brother says, the men were so close to one another, so dedicated to victory, that they took a vow of celibacy. "Not a bad idea," I tell my brother. A fly on the wall would have said we made quite a pair.

Musubi

Amanda Price

(Haruko)

The house is her battleground, a war between omission and his dead grandmother. The autumn colored rose print upholstery, meant to be for all seasons, and the avocado drapes mock the delicacy of the blues she tries to introduce into the rooms. Her hints of silver and accents of black are stars shining through a galaxy of applesauce, showing that this house was made for earth: for birthing, fried pork chops, and Bible study, things which nourish the soul. The house won't echo what-ifs or harbor unanswered questions. His grandmother still lives in the fabric of this house and she's determined her grandson will have a good wife.

I tried to teach Abbey to be a fighter, but also to recognize which rounds are won by blood and which by grace, which are worth fighting for and which are worth only walking away, but she only listened to one side. She doesn't stop fighting whether worth it or not. And I try to teach her to hold her temper, to listen, and to ignore when things can't be changed, not to fight against a structure of wood and spirit that has been in his family for generations. But she has the heart of a Yakuza, like my brother Sueyoshi, who thought he could force himself out of our caste. We're rice field workers who still speak Meiji Japanese, but I raised my son to be a shichi-dan in judo, a sensei of his own dojo. My granddaughter chose her life and now she has to live within the house she built around herself, and all I can do is advise her, if only she'd listen.

Every time I walk through the door of her house, I pause and gather strength to breathe and lift the years of strangers' memories that drape across my shoulders. Abbey's eyes are becoming those of a cornered animal but her body is tiring from the strain, like a finch battering itself against a window. She's trying to be a good wife, and I'm trying to teach her—how to clean the shower head with vinegar, how to slip a good idea into her husband's head so he thinks it came from his own mind, and especially, how to cook. Her husband has a weak stomach, upset by stress and strange food. She must learn how to hold her tongue and manage spices.

Now I'm in her house again, only the third time in this year she's been married, for dinner with her new family. She shows off her new name along with her new place settings, but in her eyes I see she's tearing like weak fabric. I see this in her face, in her motions, and in the perfection of her napkins, folded into cranes for luck. In her body, I can see she's pregnant, but this is still a secret. Her husband's mother's face reads a careful recounting of where she went wrong, wondering if letting her son watch Starblazers made him too accepting. In wartime, when my husband held my hand in public, other soldiers would yell "Johnny got a zero!" These things only made my resolve stronger, but Abbey swallows it all until she is full of bitterness. I smile, but I can still hear the soldiers.

Sakae is my real name, but I was sickly so they changed it to Haruko, a name my mother picked from a basket offered by the Buddhist priest. He said my name was overpowering me. Abbey was the name her father chose for her, after some writer who loves empty land more than people. Her father should have taken the name with him when he left, because now my granddaughter retreats into herself too often, where I have to search for her and the land is unfamiliar. Now

Abbey wants a Japanese name like her cousin Sachiko; she wants to become an instant Buddhist—add dharma and she'll fluff into something as quick and pure as those instant mashed potatoes her husband's mother brought with her. Mashed potatoes and rice at the same table, like my daughter-in-law who asked for potato chips with my teriyaki chicken.

When her husband's family is watching football and Abbey is bent over a sink of dishes, I place them on the shelves for her after I dry them. She's arranged her cupboards the same as mine, the only way she knows how, so I know where each piece rests.

"Did you ever think you'd be married forty-eight years?" she asks.

"He tells people he is tolerant, that is why we lasted so long."

She's quiet for a moment and motions toward her husband. "Do you think we will last?" And, as I pause to consider this, she breaks down. "What if I have a baby with flippers and they put it in a jar at the Smithsonian? What if I have a midget? Mom was pretty short. So are you. What if it has no chin, bad eyesight, freckles, thin hair, a long torso, short legs, weak teeth, flat feet, and allergies? What if this is punishment for my baby before?"

I put my arms around her and she folds herself into me. She's never mentioned the baby she couldn't have before, but I know she had to get rid of it and I know how guilty she feels. This was before she met her husband, before this life. She's afraid her body hasn't forgiven her and she's afraid that she'll end up like her mother, that her baby will grow up uncertain. She doesn't see that I wanted her, my grandchild, and that makes her even more valuable, even if her mother had stayed. She can't see that she'll be a good mother. She sees her unborn child in her head and she feels as heavy as granite, full of futures she needs to shape. Her arms ache for the daughter she didn't have. This house becomes a womb itself, incubating old dreams.

(Abbey)

I live in a time capsule and having my family over for dinner just makes it worse. Unearth me in 2010 when my furnishings are antique, but not before then, when this stuff is just an eyesore, something that was beautiful once and special but just looks horrid in the light twenty years later, like the way I've felt all my life. My childhood spent with Aunties hovering over me, "She's so cute! And smart! It must be the Oriental!" before Oriental became a label of the oppressors and my skim milk white Midwestern father could realize this wasn't a compliment for him. Only now at restaurants fledgling neo-Nazis sit beside me and tell me that my country doesn't want me because I'm tainted, yellow. I was born slightly jaundiced. I watch them feast on chicken-fried steak and pray for high cholesterol so all their bad karma will stampede over them and they'll return as untouchables or partially Asian women sitting alone in Denny's. Does America know all the nice things Timothy Leary said about the Japanese? Does my grandmother know her culture is held in such high esteem? Manzanar never really closed down; they just moved it to my living room.

Grandma brought what she makes best: sushi, on a lacquer plate that Grandpa carries in with pride. It really is something to admire, every shred of egg and carrot arranged according to some symbolic ancestral recipe that pleases the eye as well as the tongue. In her arms she cradles a Tupperware container filled with musubi, plump and nestled together like starchy rabbits, what we always ate for lunch on long car trips. Rice balls are my comfort food, what I associate with sustenance and my grandmother's bribery, to just hold on until we get to the next rest stop and be sure to take the Lysol in with me when I go. When she brings musubi she's after something, and I'm afraid this time, she wants my heart.

"Shrimps!" she says with the voice of a conspirator, "Did you mix the big ones in with the small ones like I say? Cheaper! No one will know!"

I absorb this knowledge and nod, trying to look humble, impressed, and appreciative all at once. "But it's shrimp."

"No! More than one! SHRIMPS!" she huffs as if four years of an American college education have produced a moron for her family, someone who can't count seafood correctly. My mother-in-law smiles in a way that sends bile racing up my throat, as if we're country-jacks and our food is a quaint diversion. Jacob smiles the smile I first liked about him and continues devouring the sushi, leading his parents into the living room to drink tea and watch the Miami Dolphins. My husband would bear Dan Marino's children if he could, and for his ability to hold such a simple, powerful devotion I love him.

Grandma likes him too or she wouldn't pour tea for him. She'd threaten to haunt me when she dies like she did when I was dating Robert. "Makes me want to vomit," she'd say. "Don't talk about him when I'm eating." For Jacob, she gives special shrimp recipes and doesn't tell him when his new haircut makes his head look small.

"He sort of looks like Zippy the Pinhead now," I said.

"Oh how cruel. Your own husband," she says and looks down shaking her head, making the clucking noise which means she failed in raising me. When I had bangs cut, cruelty didn't stop her from telling me I looked like a Japanese lantern. I walked around for months, growing out, feeling my skin stretched transparent like rice paper enveloping the moon, with my bad judgment shining through.

I watch my grandmother bring my grandfather musubi with tea, how he accepts with grace, how for forty-eight years they practice patience with each other, a love more expressive than all our public kisses, and how they still laugh.

For my wedding she folded one thousand paper cranes, for patience and luck, her gifts to me. I'm ashamed at how quickly I forgot her fingers threading wire through the wings of cranes to make streamers for me of gold, of my married future. I'm ashamed of how quickly I forget the strength of my family. We will have a baby girl and her name will be Sakae. The house will open around her to welcome her smile. I enfold Jacob with my arms and hold him, letting all of autumn fall away and one thousand cranes of luck spin circles of gold around us.

Taking Certain Measures

Paul Bowers

Saturdays are for yard work, so I rolled the commercial Toro from the tool shed, primed the carburetor, prepared to give it a smooth, firm pull, when Hargrove lifted his mug over the slat fence. "Got enough mower there, Richardson?" he said, "Bale some hay, till some taters? Would a man call such a thing overkill, Richie Rich?" I waved at him, half trying to wave him off. "When you going to give me that loan for a backyard pool, Mister Managing Loan Officer of First Bank or Bust? I'm no thoroughgoing land creature."

I adjusted the choke on my mower, measured with my fingers the precise amount to leave open to fire the engine on the first pull. I didn't feel up to sparring with him, getting caught up in his verbal acrobatics. "See Joan Simmons on Monday," I said. "Home improvement. She'll fix you up."

"Right. Simmons, Joan. Do I tell her who sent me or will that send a shudder through her silks, give her the Big Wig willies?" His face was excessively tan, skin sagging under his chin into a brown wattle.

"Doesn't matter."

"Fine and dandy," he said, slipped below the fence, only to resurface. "By the by, you and Winnie got the invite, right? A dose of anniversary cheer for me and the Missus. Already a year, you know. Tonight, seven o'clock. Goes until I say git. You coming?" I waved at him again, nodded, until he dove, disappeared for good. It was his third first anniversary party in the last five years.

I cut wide swathes through the yard. The bagger puffed like bread rising, and I stopped precisely every fourth turn to empty clippings into our compost pile. Particles of grass drifted through the air, landed on the tip of my nose, the ridges of my ears, the brush of my eyebrows. The sun fried the back of my neck, my arms ached from pushing.

At last count, Wynona had exactly one hundred and fourteen goals to reach before the end of the millennium. The first ten were pounds to lose, the last to stand at Machu Picchu, site of ancient blood sacrifices, and toast in the next thousand years with a bottle of Spanish Negro.

On my third round I thought of item thirty-seven: buy a riding lawnmower—padded cushion, five-speed, headlights, mulcher, twin bagger, emission controls, automatic kill switch. I clenched my teeth until my jaw hurt, finished the lawn in record time, smooth as a golf course, carved into neat parallel lines. A professional job.

I wiped the grimy perspiration from my face with a towel, carried a tin bucket of 10–20–10 fertilizer to my tomato patch in the corner, took a handful of dusty granules, nitrogen rich, and scattered it around the base stems of the skeletal plants.

🐎   🐎   🐎   🐎   🐎

We were already nine inches behind in rainfall for the year. The edges of my lawn turned lemon yellow, paled by drought, despite my sneaking out at midnight to water on both odd and even days, in defiance of a strict city ordinance. I noticed small cracks breaking from beneath my foundation; shallow, branching webs extending beyond the patio and creeping to meet those coming from Hargrove's yard. I measured them with a rake handle one evening, the largest nearly three inches deep, ten feet long.

And for months, along with the lack of rainfall, the monotonous blue sky, the fault lines fanning out into my lawn, the chainsaw-buzzing of locusts in my redbud, I felt a general lack of vitality, a draining away of energy in my hands, the muscles in my legs. I sat in the recliner during the evening news and covertly counted my heartbeats, felt it slow down until I had to get up and perform deep knee bends to get my circulation going.

Wynona put a multi-vitamin on the edge of my dinner plate every evening for a couple of weeks, made me swallow it while she watched. Our refrigerator was full of vegetable juice, broccoli, carrots, ripening peaches, deep purple eggplant, soft bricks of tofu. On top of the refrigerator were clusters of vitamin bottles, even a bottle of gelatinous green capsules full of fish oil, sold as smart pills. But I couldn't tell Wynona that what I felt had its origins outside my body, that I was just a barometer, a detector of odd vibrations, and that she was the real source of my disturbances, my tingling hands, weak knees, decreased heart rate, itchy skin—maybe even the drought, and our scrawny tomato plants.

It was Mr. Harrier, a retired chemist, who got me thinking, whose impromptu lecture delivered over the fence, unintentionally encouraged by my pulling weeds on that side of the yard, finally started to make sense. Hargrove calls him the Mad Scientist, and we all try to avoid him if possible. Mr. Harrier told me, staring up at a cloudless sky, scratching his silver head as if to pull up the exact computations, "We've fooled ourselves for years about weather patterns," he said. "One little wobble in convection currents, a slight shift in temperature gradients, and it'll snow in Panama. Think about it," he said, leaning over the gate so his wife wouldn't hear, "one fortuitous little fart in Kansas City at a critical moment and you've got a drought in the jungle and floods in the desert. Too many goddamned variables, and nothing ever just goes away. Laws of thermodynamics, you know. Next thing you know we're dry as a camel's asshole." He mumbled on about water tables, the great aquifers, experiments in turbulence, then lost his train of thought and slid into a quiet discussion of his granddaughter's singing lessons. "Got the pipes of a nightingale, that baby does." I nodded and pulled at what looked like budding sandburs.

🖋   🖋   🖋   🖋   🖋

I heard Hargrove on his patio, the creak of lawn chairs, Ella's soft, lazy laugh. They were sunning themselves, rejuvenating like lizards on granite. I leaned over to cup a small green tomato in my hand and caught, through a gap in the slat fence, a glimpse of their reclining nude bodies.

My tomatoes had aphids, tiny creatures that crouch on the fuzzy underside of the leaves. Wynona wouldn't let me use pesticides, so I picked them off by hand, pinched them between my fingers into little purple dots. I was trying hard to keep my mind on insects, to mind my own business, when Hargrove let out a yell. I heard the sharp scrape of aluminum on concrete, the rattle of a thin lawn chair overturned. I leaned over to peek through the gap again, watched Hargrove struggle to get up from the patio. Ella grabbed an orange towel, partially wound it around her waist, and dashed into the house. Hargrove snarled like a dog, stalked her, cradled his bottle of beer against the hump of his stomach, looked in my general direction, then slipped into the shaded cave of his living room.

I stood up quickly, brushed the dirt from my knees, struck my tingling hands together. I pulled the sprinkler into the center of the yard and opened the spigot wide. The water rose in high silver arches before shattering into wet confetti.

🖋   🖋   🖋   🖋   🖋

I battled the drought by taking frequent showers, stood hunched under the spray for long periods, until the house was drained of hot water. That evening Wynona sat in front of the mirror in her white robe, towel wound into a soft cone on her head. She put on rose eyeshadow, plucked her chin, rubbed the steamed mirror with a dry wash rag every few minutes.

"It's a classic case of Svengali Syndrome," she said. "A perverted economic nurturing. Hargrove clearly has maternal instincts." Wynona tapped into such psycho-babble with ease. When we first met, she called people she didn't like "squids." Now she required more clinical terms, influenced by talk-show shrinks.

I lathered my face, imagined a motherly Hargrove baking cookies for his new wife, tying her shoelaces.

"He channels his desire to be a mother through his checkbook. Did you hear he's sending her to business college?"

"No," I said, pictured Hargrove slipping a backpack over Ella's shoulders, kissing her on the cheek, handing her a sack lunch with a piece of fruit. "He wants a loan for a pool. I don't want to get involved but he keeps insisting."

"A symbolic return to the womb," she said.

"For Hargrove?"

"For Ella, but for Hargrove's sake. Haven't you ever noticed? He's never considered his wives as individuals, just rebirths. He recycles them. They're all the same age, with the same hair, same adolescent giggle—all pudgy little brown-eyed beauties."

I turned off the water, pushed open the shower door. "You think she's fat?"

Wynona pulled a comb through her hair, tugged hard at a tangle. "*He's* certainly getting old and flabby. The guy's scared to death he'll lose her."

"Did he tell you all this?" I asked, although I knew, the moment I opened my mouth, I should have let the subject drop. I felt the sudden pull of Wynona's lingering sadness, an emotional gravity that hollowed out my bones—a phenomenon that began the day she opened my corporate Visa bill and discovered a charge for a hotel room downtown when I was supposed to be two hundred miles away at a business conference. I think the root of her quiet anger was less a matter of my infidelity than the idiotic simplicity of it, my disappointing lack of creativity, the ease of the discovery.

Analyzing the neighbors, her brother, my parents, kept our own problems at bay, although I felt the pressure building against us, against me, and I wasn't really surprised when the thin wall between my sins and her anger began to bulge. What I didn't anticipate was her subtlety, such a careful measuring of retribution yet to come.

"He never says anything directly," Wynona finally answered, "but he doesn't have to. You don't think Hargrove's throwing just another anniversary party, do you? This time he wants it to stick so he has to make it extremely public, in front of the people who know him best. I feel sorry for Ella."

Wynona was right—Hargrove was always throwing parties, but he made quite a fuss over this one. But I said, "Seems innocent enough."

"Only to the uninitiated," she said, then clicked on the hair dryer.

🐎　🐎　🐎　🐎　🐎

A blue catering truck took up Hargrove's driveway, rear to the garage. I peeked through the bedroom blinds at a short muscular woman who wore blue jeans, an orange tank top, tan Mule gloves. She shuttled boxes back and forth, one crowded with champagne bottles like gold-tipped bowling pins. Only the best for Mother Hargrove's prodigy, I thought, believing that she, too, would grow tired of him like her predecessors, leave him in a drunken stupor on his patio.

Wynona coated her hair with a fine mist of hair spray, held her nose to avoid the fumes. "Hargrove is self-destructing before our very eyes, the last of a dying breed." I imagined Hargrove sinking into the soft sand of a riverbed, lying on his side, gradually covered with alluvial sediments, fossilized into sandstone.

"What did we get them?" I asked, tried to find my already Scotch-numbed tongue, tightened my belt around my thinning waist.

"A two-handled coffee mug with a hand-painted heart in the middle."

"Sounds a little cheap," I said. "What did we get him for his last first anniversary?"

Wynona pat under her chin with the back of her hand. "Earthen dinnerware with Inca engravings. You picked it out, remember? He melted them in the dishwasher."

I sucked on an ice cube that tasted like mouthwash and checked my socks for holes. "Figures."

🐖 🐖 🐖 🐖 🐖

We had been to Hargrove's little gatherings before. At Christmas his house smelled of cinnamon potpourri, in spring, rose, in summer, pine. He marked the passage of time with smells and ex-wives. It was a little past seven and the Montgomerys walked in ahead of us—Nick and Marsha, husband-and-wife real estate partners. Hargrove blocked the foyer until Marsha, wearing a khaki dress and brown boots, took off her scarved pith helmet and kissed his thick neck. "Enter Bwana," he said, "and your faithful porter." He took a bottle of Zinfandel from Nick. "I see you left that poodle of yours at home."

"Boarded for the night," Nick said.

"At the Ritz, no doubt."

I gave Nick a friendly pat on the back, encouraged him to move along so I could get out of the heat. He turned sideways, squeezed between Hargrove and a sprawling potted tree.

"Ah," Hargrove said, opening his arms wide. "My next-door Richardsons. Glad to get out of the fields for a while, give the dandelions a chance in hell?"

"A slight respite," I slurred. Hargrove looked at me, then stooped to whisper in Wynona's ear.

She nodded knowingly. "Right after he came out of the shower. He tripped over the welcome mat on the way in."

"Primed the pump, eh?" Hargrove lifted my hand, pressing it lightly. "I used to chug a beer or two just before going to confession. Loosened the tongue a bit, you know? Made life much more interesting for the good Father."

"Always thinking of others," I said.

"It's the Christian way."

Wynona pulled me by the arm, guiding me into the den toward the Pinkneys. Loren Pinkney wore a light gray sportcoat, one hand stuffed in his pants pocket; the other scooped a cracker into his mouth. He saw us coming, wiped his fingers on a shredded napkin tucked in his shirt collar. "Evening," he mumbled.

Rachel Pinkney, her graying hair wound into a hard, metallic bun, fingered Wynona's sleeve. "What a beautiful dress. Isn't it too warm?" Wynona shook her head.

Loren Pinkney limply grasped my hand. "Seems we've done this before," he said in a low voice. "We brought a coffee table book on Picasso. Blue period. You?"

"A mug of some sort." Loren opens his eyes wide during conversations, caterpillar-eyebrows lifting nearly to his hairline. I never could look him in the eye without being drawn to his forehead. "Wynona picked it up somewhere," I said.

"The book was a virtual freebee. Buy five, get one for a penny. Fifty dollar value, though." His voice trailed off.

"Here goes it," Hargrove said, handing me a glass of Scotch. "Fresh-squeezed."

Ella came from the open kitchen and stood beside him.

He draped his arm across her shoulders. She smiled at me and I raised my glass. "Congratulations," I said, then took a sip. She tried to put her arm around Hargrove's thick waist, but settled for a pat on his back. She wore a white satin dress, sleeveless, exposing strong brown arms, her hair braided into a tight rope that ended in a slender white bow. I tried to guess her age—twenty-two, maybe twenty-five. "And good luck to you both," I said, lifted my glass again and dribbled Scotch down the front of my shirt. Ella quickly took a napkin from a serving tray, dabbed at my chest.

"I thought even you were beyond dribble glasses," Loren said.

"Not me," Hargrove insisted, raising his hand in oath. "Richardson here just has faulty lips."

Ella's long fingernails scratched through the napkin. The back of my neck tingled. "There's food in the den," she said, wadding the wet napkin, slyly tucking it into Hargrove's pants pocket. "I'll put on some music."

Hargrove looked at me, winked, felt for the napkin in his pocket. "A tidy one, she is."

"Very," I said before I could think, then shot a quick glance at Wynona. But she turned away to quiz Rachel about her new job in the mayor's office.

Cecil Burke had the Montgomerys backed against the cold fireplace. They nodded frequently, looked concerned while Cecil asked if the time was right to buy into a frozen burrito business. The Normans, Eddie and Irene, sat on the love seat below them, looking cramped, afraid Cecil would spill his plate of shrimp wontons in their laps.

When the music began, a hard run of booming drums that grew in volume, everyone was startled. "What exactly is that?" Wynona asked Hargrove.

"Something Ella likes," he said. "African drum sonatas, or some such thing."

Wynona listened, moved her head in rhythm like she was savoring some exotic spice on the back of her tongue. She tends to overdo such things. "It's different."

"I suppose you have to have an ear for it," Loren said, lifting his eyebrows.

Rachel squinted, a reflex action against the noise. The wrinkles under her eyes deepened and multiplied, despite her attempt to fill them in with a thick layer of peach-colored face powder.

"Ella spends a good afternoon at the mall at least once a month. God knows where she gets the stuff," Hargrove said, digging a finger in his ear. "I find the La-Z-Boy showroom and take a catnap."

"You let her go play with the credit card?" Wynona asked.

Hargrove nodded. "I wander into the bookstore sometimes, look at the girlie magazines. First-rate journalism, you know. She comes and puts me on a leash when she's done." Hargrove turned away, nodded across the room. "There's a study for you."

Alice North, a pediatric nurse, short-winded from twenty years of smoking, danced around the coffee table with her boyfriend. I tried to think of his name. Long black hair pulled into a tight ponytail, round-lens glasses. Always wore green socks. Rock, or Rocky, or Robby.

Hargrove poured me a refill of Chivas, said, "She's been trolling the nursing school again I see, taking temperatures."

"He's a nurse?" Loren Pinkney asked.

"More like a Norse, if you take her word for it."

"What's his name?" I asked, a little too loudly.

Hargrove said, "Bolt Upright, I would imagine," and everyone laughed.

Ella brought another tray, wheat crackers and pate,

carrot and celery sticks speared into a bowl of french onion dip. Loren laced vegetables through his fingers, shuffled through crackers with his free hand. When he couldn't come up with anything else he wanted, he gestured toward a desert landscape painting over the couch, lifted his eyebrows, chewed like a contented bull. "Always up-to-date, huh Hargrove? It's been dry this year."

"Less than two inches of rain in the last three months," I said, trying to raise a level of alarm. "I heard on the evening news that the Sahara is expanding twenty feet a year, swallows up everything green. Other places have too much rain, though. Five hundred killed in a landslide in Bangladesh." I kept the gruesome details to myself, the images I saw on TV. Many hung on for hours, up to their chins in mud, until the breath was squeezed out of them. Relatives find them too late, squat in a silent circle around the head of an aunt or uncle, while other villagers wander by, whistling for lost goats.

"Do tell," Loren mumbled through a mouthful of cracker. "Makes me hot just thinking about it."

"Go outside at three in the afternoon and you'll feel what hot is," I said.

"All of us don't share your passion for growing things." He cleared his throat. "You grow grass, right?" Rachel let out a laugh like Woody Woodpecker.

"Richardson cultivates," Hargrove interjected, "and we're all the better for it."

"It's a beautiful lawn," Ella said. "You don't get green like that by just waiting for it to happen."

"He's a fanatic," Wynona said.

"A master gardener in a suburban wasteland," Hargrove added. "He was giving the place a tender manicure just this afternoon. I saw him squeezing his tomatoes."

Then I felt Ella's hand on my arm. She smiled shyly. "I hope we didn't embarrass you today. We were just being silly."

Hargrove knotted his hand into a fist, lightly tapped my chin with his thick knuckles. "Damn right," he said. "It's a wonder you don't have us arrested."

Wynona scooped a piece of ice from her glass, sounded like she was crunching her words, "Did we miss something here?"

"Nothing much," Hargrove said. "We were just acting out a little scene on the patio. We were adrift in the Adriatic in two small boats—lawn chairs in this case. We discover an island, the story goes, uninhabited, with coconut groves surrounding a lagoon. Real *Gilligan's Island* stuff. And the question of the day was, would two consenting adults of the opposite persuasion, finding themselves in that position, really wear clothes to sunbathe? Unfortunately, as Richardson here knows, the answer is nay, thou shalt not be swaddled."

"In the buff?" Loren asked me.

"I don't know," I lied. "I just heard something."

"That was the sound of Ella panicking," Hargrove said. "We've got to fix that fence. It seems when the wife saw Richardson tending his crops she dove for cover and ruined the whole scene. Tough to recover the milieu."

"It was silly," Ella repeated.

Wynona started pawing at her hair, adjusted the neckline of her dress, cleared her throat, and said, without looking at me, "Had fun today, did we? No wonder I can't get him out of the yard."

"We aim to please," Hargrove said.

I felt a tug at my ankles, the weight of a stone in my stomach.

〰 〰 〰 〰 〰

Wynona took charge of the gifts, bullied her way past Marsha Montgomery, handed the presents to Ella one at a time like she was feeding a starving animal, made her beg for every morsel. But by nine o'clock, nearly everything was unwrapped: a book on Picasso, a set of stemware, a two-year subscription to *National Geographic*, carved wooden elephants heavy enough for bookends, a videotape collection of *The Honeymooners*. Ella arranged the gifts in a circle around her, bowed slightly like a queen holding court.

Wynona kept our present behind her until everything else was open, then produced an oddly shaped package, wrapped in a bold pink print that read *Happy Anniversary*!

Ella took it awkwardly and carefully removed the wrapping paper, folding it neatly into a square in her lap. She shuffled through wadded newspaper and dug her hand into the box. I expected to see the glint of ceramic, but out of the box came a small paperback. I found myself staring at the black and white cover photo of a dark-haired woman with big glasses.

"What is it?" Loren Pinkney asked, looking at me, probably wondering why I lied about the present.

I knew something was up by the way Ella held the book to her face. She looked quickly to Hargrove, then Wynona, then me. "*How to Make Your Man Happy: 100 Everyday Things You Can Do to Keep Him*," she said.

Hargrove suddenly stiffened, shot a glance my way, the last remnants of his smile turned to clay—and for a brief instant, a fleeting look of sadness, eyes of a frightened man peering out from the overly-tanned face of one who had suffered through two divorces in four years. We all came to his anniversary party to aid him in his performance, help him erect a facade of stability. And we all knew, though perhaps had not taken seriously, how hard he worked to make this marriage appear as prosperous as all the other aspects of his life, not to let this one crumble around him. But Wynona, flagrantly breaking rank, deliberately out of step with the supporting cast, decided to save Ella instead.

Wynona said, "It's by Dr. Laurie Anderson," as if everyone would recognize the name. "Not too clinical, not too patronizing. It's really about power relations in a marriage—who has it, who doesn't."

"I hope that's a hundred recipes," Hargrove said, recovering quickly, patting his round stomach. "The way to a man's heart and all that."

"Self-help books are big sellers," Rachel Pinkney said, nodding at Ella.

"Yes," a few mumbled in assent. I picked at a loose strand of carpet.

Ella stood up, moved around the room to thank everyone with a kiss on the cheek. Wynona leaned over to take ours.

🐏   🐏   🐏   🐏   🐏

Hargrove served us all slices of lemon cake on red paper plates and poured glasses of sweet champagne. We arranged ourselves in an irregular circle. Cecil Burke squatted on the floor, pressed cake crumbs with his fingers. Alice North parked herself on her boyfriend's lap and teased his ponytail. The Montgomerys sat on the love seat, backs stiff, listening to Hargrove complain about property taxes. Eddie and Irene Norman took off each other's shoes. Irene pushed them under the coffee table, reached down from the couch every few minutes to fiddle with Eddie's shoelaces. Wynona ate silently, pushed a crumbling piece of cake from one edge of the plate to the other, squirmed against the cushions of the couch.

The lemon cake and Scotch turned to acid in my stomach, so I got up to go to the bathroom, but made it only so far as Hargrove's bed. I stretched out on my back for a moment, but kept my eyes open, anchored myself to the mattress so I wouldn't fall into the dark whirlpool that started in my head and spiraled into my legs.

I could tell the room really belonged to Ella—pink and powder blue, the air sweet with perfume. She took over where the others left off, marked her territory with family photos and a fresh coat of paint. She must have scrubbed the room, disinfected everything to get rid of their smells, vacuumed up the long hairs tangled in the carpet. On the nightstand, next to the phone, was a hardback book, *Introduction to Business,* and a green stenographer's pad.

Nothing belonged to Hargrove, as if he voluntarily eradicated any traces of himself, let Ella turn the bedroom into her sanctuary. Wynona was preaching to the converted, I thought.

I got off the bed carefully, tried not to wrinkle the comforter, and staggered into the bathroom. The sink counter swam with blue and red fish soap. I turned on the cold water and splashed my face. I took my time, knew that Wynona was waiting for me to come back, so I pulled up my pants, tucked in my shirt, then pulled the tail out again and started over. I looked in the mirror, began by smoothing down my cowlick with a little water, and spent a good half hour rearranging myself and thinking how Wynona had got us both, me and Hargrove. That was how she thought of us, cut from the same cloth, both a little stiff in the knees, pompous, both scared as hell, both sinners.

When I went back to the living room, they were all just as I left them. Loren Pinkney worked on another piece of cake, though with little gusto, everyone watching him maneuver yet one more bite into his gaping mouth. Wynona turned to me, her eyes drunk and angry. I dropped beside her on the couch and Hargrove said,

"You find the chamber pot all right, Richardson?" I nodded. "You know, in the old days, a true gentleman would place his foot in the pot and let urine trickle down his leg so as not to wake his lady."

I gave Wynona a little nudge with my elbow, but she didn't respond. "You know, Winnie's got a list of things to do before the end of the millennium."

"A list?" Irene Norman asked, producing a low-key yawn. Eddie Norman took it up, stretched his legs, looked at the watch strapped on his hairy arm.

But Hargrove ignored all the signs of fatigue and said, "Let's hear it."

Wynona let out a deep gush of air, looked up at the ceiling as if struggling to remember all one hundred and fourteen items. But I knew she tilted her head back to keep the tears from falling, and was ready to stomp out of the room, leaving me on the couch like I left her, surrounded.

To my surprise, she started the list, skipping the first ten about pounds, and beginning with eleven. "Pretty modest stuff really. Read a book a month. Buy fresh flowers once a week. See all of Bogart's movies. Have more candlelight dinners. Learn to dance—" She paused.

"Go on," Ella said.

"Eat more fruit. Exercise regularly. Clean out the attic. Practice patience. Start a scrapbook. Paint the house."

I looked down at the floor while Wynona spoke with the steadiness of a ticking clock, gathering herself into each item before she let it go into the room. I felt a surge of energy emanating from her, looked up to record the expressions of pity on all those faces, saw them all involuntarily gravitate toward her, drawn like planets around a collapsing star.

I scooted nearer the couch arm, tried to gain a measure of comfortable distance, a margin of safety.

The next morning Wynona was still in bed at eleven o'clock, tangled in the sheets like a tuna in a gill net. I sat at the kitchen table, drank coffee, tried to keep my aching head still. I usually woke her before nine on Sundays, read the entertainment section to her in bed, then went to McDonald's for a take-out of biscuits and sausage gravy. But I knew neither of us would be up for breakfast, so I didn't even bother trying to find my car keys.

I thought we could pass the day apart, maintain a disciplined silence like faithful monks, leave for work Monday morning in separate cars, meet for a late lunch at Fat Jack's, and try to re-negotiate our marriage over corned beef sandwiches and dill pickle wedges. But I realized she would make up an excuse—too tired, too tense, too hurt—take the blame on herself, and try to draw me so deeply into her sorrow I'd never come out of it.

As it turned out, I had little say in the matter anyway. She took a leave of absence from her job, went to stay with her brother in Atlanta. I hadn't heard from her for nearly a month when she finally called, asked if I'd mind sending her the registration for her car. "I'm thinking of selling it," she said flatly.

"Do you need money?"

"God no," she said and hung up.

Hargrove had a rowdy work crew digging a pool in his yard, and when Wynona called a second time a few days later to tell me she changed her mind about selling her car, I could barely hear her over the roar of the backhoe. At first she simply talked louder, asked that I send her a few books. Then, calmly, "They're putting in the pool?"

"All week," I said. "Morning, noon, and night."

There was a short pause, a little laugh breaking through. "Good for them," she said.

That day the sun set a brilliant orange. *Red sky at night, sailor's delight,* I thought. I threw myself into the patio chaise lounge and watched the sprinkler soak the ground well into the night.

And still, after nearly two months, my recovery efforts have had little effect. But I hope to worry my lawn back to health before winter, force a slight change in direction that will prove the decisive turning point. I wait for the first real sign that something good will come of it all.

Song of So

Brooks Tower

Mine own Vinyard Have I Not Kept

S
o, let's say I write this story for the anthology, and let's say it's accepted. Matter of fact, let's say the judge likes it so much he/she/they even call(s) me up to talk about it, even buy(s) my lunch, even offer(s) to have sex with me, and all of them let me drive their car(s).

Some of the other stories are okay, too.

And I'm sitting in Medina's a couple of days after it's published, cooling the sweat of my brow after an afternoon of respectable toil over at the Walker garden, and an old acquaintance is telling me how much he enjoyed the story—really—how he's glad I started writing again—and this young woman sitting at the next table overhears and asks did you write that story? and I say yeh, and she says, your mouth is most sweet; yea, you are altogether lovely—

wait, no—

"Hey," she says, "are you that guy?" And yeah, I saith unto her, I am that guy. So we get to talking, and she's a painter—no, a potter, and lo, she has educated, beautiful hair, intelligent eyes, silky conversation, nice bottom, breasts like twin young roes that feed among the lilies.

Her name is Rachael, say. She has a young son from a disastrous first marriage to some asshole oilie—I think I've actually met the guy. Her laughter is like sorghum. She has a dog. And me, I'm actually forming words into intelligent sentences, asking questions, approaching even unto suaveness.

No, no, never happen—but maybe my acquaintance,

maybe he asks her—and she answers him while looking at me. And this guy—he's really my best friend, almost—he tells her about my gardens and my funky house—and I stay kind of awkward, diffident, and I can tell she likes that. And turns out she gardens too. Turns out she reads! And no, she also doesn't understand how people can ignore what's happening, everywhere, now, half of all Creation disappearing in our lifetimes, in a geological instant . . .

Tree huggers in love, we stare into each other's cassandraic eyes, and I haven't even mentioned my ex even once, and I can tell—even weird, paranoid me—I can tell she's intrigued, wants to know more.

"Hey," she says, "is that your car out front with the bumper sticker? The 'I heart my dick' one?" Pause, two, three, I deny it. Her eyes narrow. We achieve flirtation.

But then she asks what I do.

"And so are you a landscape architect or something? A teacher?" and I clear my throat in preparation to explaining to her that no, not exactly, no, actually that's what could be called a major contradiction in my life—but my table mate blurts out—laughingly blurts out—

"Ha! Are you kidding? He works for an oil company just like your ex—even has to drive 200 miles just to do it." Oh fine. Oh good.

"Weird, huh?" he adds, bobbing his head in agreement with himself.

Well, that brings her up short. She looks at me and her mouth goes a little sad. "Is it true?" her eyes inquire. "Yes, and even worse" my eyes reply, before I can stop them. "Oh," she says. She returns to her table.

There is nothing new under the sun. That night I watch sitcoms and I get older.

But just you hide and watch, I will rise now, pretty soon here, and I will go about the city in the streets, and in the broad ways I will seek her whom my soul loveth.

But, I digress.

Take us the Little Foxes that Spoil the Vines

So I write this story, or, actually I've just started it, when the second bomb hits OKC.

All my gardens evaporate, and I die, so I never finish it, but its inspired scraps change the world, years later.

The second bomb's much bigger than the first. Actually, it's a thermofuckingnuclear device, accidentally set off by a psychotic Sooner fan/lawn devotee with shadowy ties to the Ukraine. (Ol' Ronnie was going to take out the evil empire—Washington, D.C.—more because of those goddamn Redskins than the ATF—but, whoops, after he hid the homemade bomb Sergei gave him in his backyard, he went and nicked it with his weed eater in his weekly subduing-the-frontier frenzy. And, in quick strokes, before the U. of S. realizes that once again, one of its own has done the Very Bad Thing, 23 missiles fly—a demi-apocalypse.)

Then many more bad things happen, nearly all at once.

The Ten Million Year Sorrow commences. (Yes, Capitalized. Yes, Ten Million.)

Humans didn't really need the added oomph that the missile shower gave us toward the Ten Million Year Sorrow. We were gamboling our way there pretty quick just by the sheer weight of numbers. (A new Philadelphia every day, a new Mexico every year . . . .) All the missiles did, they just speeded things up a little.

But, I wander.

When the federal building bomb went off, Rachael had been teaching a little geography to her fourth graders.

"Whoa!" little Jerome Benthal yelled, "What the fuck was that?" And she wanted to correct him, kept meaning to over the next 90 seconds or so, but whatever it was—such an explosion—whatever it was, was so big . . . then one of the other teachers calls her out to the hall, tells her what she's just heard on the radio, and all day the news just keeps getting bigger—the sirens, the sirens—who do I know that might have been . . . ? She never does get around to telling Jerome that little boys don't get to use words like that in her classroom.

When the second bomb blows, Rachael is out hiking in the Wichitas. She's taken my meager story scraps with her, and she's just read them and been rather eye-openingly under-impressed. Well, huh, she thinks, this is going to be uncomfortable—trying to give this back to him without having to say what I think about it—and, then, behind her, to the northeast, OKC becomes a brief second sun.

Over the next few years, as the natural world swiftly collapses around her, she accidentally saves these few precious words of her almost lover—don't ask me how; I'm already dead—and she gives them to her soon-to-be culted son, Isaiah, who three years later is baptised in the radioactive shallows of the North Canadian, baptised into the new, much shorter life of the Glowing One by some idiot named Juan.

And my few ill-thought out phrases and plot lines, loaned to a young woman in hopes of effecting a 19th century seduction by words, they become the next sacred text.

And all I was hoping for, really, was a nice turn of phrase.

But, I deconstruct . . .

A Good Name Is Better than Precious Ointment.

So, I think about writing this story, only I don't, but the ex writes one. It's amateurish and trendy—but everybody loves it anyway and she gets famous, and . . .

Wait, no, she writes it about me! She lies! Everyone hates me! It wasn't like that! You weren't there!

But, I convulse.

Jealousy Is as Cruel as the Grave

So, I'm thinking about writing this story, driving down to see ol' Combo in Bricktown, but when I get there, *she* is there—oh, and *her* too, and all thoughts of any kind of meaningful communication or writing the next Bible, or anything, just dissolve.

Him, too, he's there. And several of *them,* all sitting together.

My personal history drives me from the place. I decide to move.

I do move. I move to Costa Rica, and Rachael goes with me, Rachael and Isaiah, and I work as a janitor/cook/handyman at a rainforest lodge until I'm bitten—no, shot, by a brown man with an angry vision.

But, I ramble.

I Sleep but my Heart Waketh

So I'm reading the anthology to which a story I really should have submitted—but you didn't, did you?—and, about it, I really am giving myself hell. Lo, and out my front window I see a dog lying in my front yard. I already have two dogs. Old dogs. Big wussy dogs. Worthless. Bad dogs. I don't need another one.

But front yard dog is bleeding, so I have to go out there and do something. It's a big mutt with curly hair. Someone has carved the name "Rachael" on its side. It looks up at me in fear and resignation.

"Geesh," I ask, "what happened to you?" Its eyes get sad. It looks away.

And so, I acquire yet another dog. I take her into the vet and she heals quickly but the scars stay. No amount of therapy helps.

I name her "Rachael."

Turns out, she is not a bad dog, no, not really—and pretty, too. Very pretty. Behold, my dog has hair like a flock of goats that appear from Mount Gilead. Smart, too. Only one bad habit—she likes to dig in my gardens. Is kind of obsessed with digging in my gardens. Feels she has no choice. Thinks it her duty. Figures it her right.

And so one day I take her with me over to my new garden. I turn my attention to the asparagus bed, and she immediately goes after a small, newly planted apricot tree. Digs it up, of course, but then keeps digging. Digs and digs. Makes a subsoil statement. Spelunks.

And behold, she digs up a pottery shard with a strange being on it, wearing what *very clearly appears to be . . . a helmut! a space helmut!*

"Jesus! Rachael!" I exclaim, not really expecting either of them to respond, "do you know what this looks like?"

"Of course I do, you idjit," she growls. Jesus remains mute for the nonce. "I planted the shard there. I mean, I put it there, but it is authentic—it really is an early American pottery shard and it really does depict people in space helmuts. It really does. But it's just not from this area." A pause as she pants a bit, licks a spot on her foreleg. "Nothing's ever from around here," she adds as she sits down and scratches at her ear mites.

"Except suffering."

Suddenly she breaks off scratching to dash after a squirrel that has pushed the critical distance-to-tree envelope a little too far.

"Something about those furry little shits—I don't know . . ." she mutters as she trots back. She turns and barks at it once as it scolds her, then shakes herself. "Actually, I found that shard near Santa Fe. They have really cool stuff there. Hey, wanna play bite-bite?"

"Rachael," says I, "how is it you never spoke to me before? And why did you play so dumb about housebreaking?"

Her ears surge forward. "It was a test, dumbshit."

"Well, then you flunked, honey, because I never saw a harder dog to—"

"It was a test of you, monkeyhead," she almost snarls. "To see if you were really worthy."

"Am I?" and "Worthy of what?" both try to come out of my mouth at the same time. Make no sense.

"Yes, you are" and "Of carrying the message to the rest of the chimps" both do come out of her mouth at the same time, although from opposite sides. The startling effect castanedas my brain more or less right down the middle, just as the giant spaceship is landing behind her. I notice there is no engine roar, hum, whine, or rattle, just soft approximation of muzak. The lights are pretty fractals.

And, turns out, this is their first stop on a world tour. OKC. Even before Santa Fe. Even before Dallas.

Beings descend from the craft. Rachael turns and wags her tail at them. After they hop over, she gives their crotches a friendly little sniff—at least I think those were their crotches. Then she makes introductions.

Eventually, after many pleasantries, they finally get around to politely asking, but I just as politely, yet firmly, refuse, so I am not probed. Even so, they do leave me the cd's they originally offered as bribes to let them do the probe thing. I have listened to them. I understand now. I know everything.

If you want to know where to hear me live, long "i," tour dates can be found at www.homogenene.me. Click on the shepherd.

But if you want to hear me live, short "i," that is much harder. Is it this buzzing in my ears? Is it the sound of me raking leaves, yesterday, along the sidewalk in the last few minutes of January evening daylight? Is it that sigh that escaped me when you closed the door behind you, that last time, that one last time?

Come, come into my garden.

So I'm writing this story when I suddenly realize that, whoops, no, I'm not writing this story, not at all. I'm not even holding a pen, there's no keyboard anywhere, no paper, . . . wait! I'm naked! And some, some woman, big woman, is giving me a sponge bath. The water is tepid, the sponge soft, but her hand is too firm. Wait, what smells so bad?—like, oh no, Jesus! It's me! I have shit on me! I have shit on my hands! No, wait, those are liver spots, wait, wait . . .

My memory has become like unto even the Everglades. Vast and meandering, fetid. Drying up. Flocks of ibises erupt into the sky of my awareness, and I am startled. Their sudden flight confuses me.

The name tag says Rachael. Pretty name, just like yours, Rachael.

Or Rochelle, something like that. Anyway she looks kind of like you. Except you had red hair. Yes? Red? Kind of brownish red? And a little mole right . . .

And I'm putting it all down in this story, see, so that there will be a record, you see, of what happened, so that people will know, so that the future will not forget the past, so that,

Oh! Very nice! Outside is very nice. I always loved the backyard, especially the—

Wait, this isn't my backyard, not at all, not even close, what is this place, Rachael?

She sighs, smiles at me, touches my arm. "Yes it is, Dad. It's your backyard."

Oh, no, it isn't. Mine has an arbor, and where's the fig? And my apples? She looks at me and she looks tired. You never had a garden, Dad. You worked too hard. You had a yard, remember? Grass?

But what does she know, Rachael? How can I remember things that never were? Your love was better than wine. Where was she when you and I, Rachael, you and I, we snuck into our garden late that summer night and made love amongst the basil, its scent perfuming the air around us? And how can she explain this dirt beneath my nails, my aching back, my sun-leathered skin?

This bare wasteland, this backyard, it cannot be mine. My life is not a lawn. My love is not tidy, is not edged.

The deserts—the parking lots, the ball games, the evangelizing, clearcutting, sentimentalizing teevee deserts—every day shift further, drying and smothering the oases of our love and memory. How can we save our garden from their sands, Rachael?

She looks at me and I see sorrow in her eyes. "We need to get you back inside, Mr. Tower," she says. "I think you've had another accident."

I think I had another life.

Make haste, my beloved, make haste . . .

Biographies

Benjamin Bates

Born and raised in Chicago, IL., Benjamin Bates attended Yale University (B.A.), The University of Iowa (M.F.A.), and Southern Illinois University-Carbondale (Ph.D.). He moved to Oklahoma in 1996 to join the faculty at Langston University, where he is chairman of the English Department.

Paul Bowers

Paul Bowers was born in Houston, Texas, but grew up in Sand Springs. He earned a B.A. in English from the University of Tulsa, and M.A. and Ph.D. degrees in English from Oklahoma State University. He is a former Associate Editor of *Cimarron Review,* and currently serves as an Assistant Professor of English at Phillips University in Enid. In addition to critical essays and book reviews, he has published fiction in a number of literary journals, including *Indiana Review* and *Mid-American Review.*

Paul Burke

Born in Boston and raised in Enid and Oklahoma City, Paul Burke currently resides in Oklahoma City. He earned a degree in English from Oklahoma City University after less inspired travels through music school and journalism classes. He has worked for the last four years for a courier company—who says you can't get a job with an English degree? He has had fiction and a critical paper published in OCU's literary magazine, *The Scarab.*

Steffie Corcoran

An Oklahoma City native, Steffie Corcoran earned a B.A. in English from Oklahoma State University and subsequently an M.A. in the same department (with a creative writing component). She is now in her fourth year of teaching seventh grade English at Del Crest Junior High School and will teach an eighth and ninth grade creative writing class for the first time this spring. She has for several years also served as contributing editor for *Oklahoma Today* magazine. She is single (and available), childless, but shares her home with an exceptional mixed-breed terrier named Ruby.

Jim Drummond

Born in Stillwater, Jim Drummond grew up in Madill and St. Louis, Missouri. He earned a B.A. in English from Wesleyan University in 1969. He earned a law degree from the University of Oklahoma in 1976 as well as earning a M.A. in Creative Writing from CCNY. He has two novels in progress. He currently works writing appeals and doing evidentiary hearings in district court for indigent clients on death row.

Christopher Forrest Givan

Born in Washington, D.C., Christopher Givan earned a
B.A. from Yale and a Ph.D. from Stanford and has since
taught at the University of California, Santa Barbara, Yale,
University of Puerto Rico, and Eastern New Mexico
University. In addition, he was awarded two Fulbrights, one
to teach in Romania and one to teach in Hong Kong.
Currently, he is a professor at the University of Central
Oklahoma in the Department of Creative Studies. He is the
author of two poetry chapbooks, "Thank You for Asking,"
and "The Sunset that Was Vanessa." He lives on an acreage
west of Guthrie with two dalmations and two cats.

Robert Hibbard

Born in Ada, Oklahoma, Robert Hibbard earned an
English degree from the University of Central Oklahoma in
the fall of 1996 and is currently employed in the university's
communications/publications office. He lives in Edmond
with his wife, Alicia, and son, Preston, who's 16 months old.

Laura Holcomb McNatt

Born in Buffalo, Oklahoma, Ms. McNatt graduated from
the University of Oklahoma and has done graduate work in
writing at the University of Oklahoma and Wichita State
University. She lives in Oklahoma City with her husband
Dan and has four children and four grandchildren.

Joan K. Moore

Joan K. Moore earned a B.A. in English and a M.A. in English with Creative Writing Emphasis from the University of Central Oklahoma where she teaches composition and a course in contemporary women writers. She is Consulting Editor for NEWPLAINS Publishing Group. She has had poetry and fiction published in *NEWPLAINS Review*, and poetry in CSWI 1996 Intercollegiate Poetry Anthology. She is currently at work on a collection of short stories, and co-editing *Miscellany*, a poetry anthology.

Amanda Price

A native of California, Amanda Price is currently enrolled as an undergraduate English major at the University of Central Oklahoma. She was the winner of the 1996 James Axley Creative Writing Award for Poetry at Rose State College, as well as a merit award in fiction. Her poems have been published or are forthcoming in *Potpourri, Poetry Motel, Chaminade Literary Review*, and *Zuzu's Petals Quarterly Online*. Ms. Price lives in Bethany with her husband and dog.

Linda Marshall Sigle

Linda Marshall Sigle was born in Schenectady, New York and is a graduate student in the Creative Studies program at the University of Central Oklahoma. She was a semi-finalist in the Writer's Network Screenwriting Competition for her screenplay, *Hitchhiking the River*, and a finalist in the Love Creek One Act Play contest for *At the Rubydoo* which was performed Off-Broadway at the Harold Clurman Theatre in New York City. Linda, who has a twelve-year-old son, Avery, lives in the woods somewhere east of Stillwater near an illegal sewage lagoon.

Brooks Tower

Brooks Tower, born in Washington, D.C., earned a degree in English from the University of Oklahoma. He is a leading proponent of the school of landscape design known as "garden noire." After 17 years as a computer analyst, he is returning to O.U. this fall to learn about plants. Previous published writings include "Impeach Gaylord" bumper sticker in 1980, several crackpot letters to the editors of various papers, and a self-published novel which he doesn't want to talk about, except to say that everybody makes mistakes.